"I want you to marry me."

Shannon's eyes widened in shock. "Marry? As in wedding?"

"Yes, Shannon."

"As in white lace and happily every after?"

Smiling, Mitch nodded.

"As in what people do before they get divorced?"

His smile flattened. "I never thought of it quite that way."

"What about the children?"

"They adore you." His eyes glowed softly.

"What about the custody fight?" she persisted.

"Don't worry. I'll handle it."

Shannon saw a quick flare of anger in Mitch's eyes. "The Gilberts have filed suit, haven't they," she said softly.

"It doesn't matter. Once we're married, they'll have lost their only weapon against me."

Shannon went white. Mitch was talking calmly, as though he hadn't just stabbed her in the heart....

Dear Reader;

This year marks our tenth anniversary and we're having a celebration! To symbolize the timelessness of love, as well as the modern gift of the tenth anniversary, we're presenting readers with a DIAMOND JUBILEE Silhouette Romance title each month, penned by one of your favorite Silhouette Romance authors.

Spend February—the month of lovers—in France with *The Ambassador's Daughter* by Brittany Young. This magical story is sure to capture your heart. Then, in March, visit the American West with Rita Rainville's *Never on Sundae*, a delightful tale sure to put a smile on your lips—and bring ice cream to mind!

Victoria Glenn, Annette Broadrick, Peggy Webb, Dixie Browning, Phyllis Halldorson—to name just a few—have written DIAMOND JUBILEE titles especially for you.

And that's not all! In March we have a very special surprise! Ten years ago, Diana Palmer published her very first romances. Now, some of them are available again in a three-book collection entitled DIANA PALMER DUETS. Each book will have two wonderful stories plus an introduction by the author. Don't miss them!

The DIAMOND JUBILEE celebration, plus special goodies like DIANA PALMER DUETS, is Silhouette Books' way of saying thanks to you, our readers. We've been together for ten years now, and with the support you've given to us, you can look forward to many more years of heartwarming, poignant love stories.

I hope you'll enjoy this book and all of the stories to come. Come home to romance—Silhouette Romance—for always!

Sincerely,

Tara Hughes Gavin
Senior Editor

DIANA WHITNEY

A Liberated Man

Silhouette *Romance*

Published by Silhouette Books New York

America's Publisher of Contemporary Romance

SILHOUETTE BOOKS
300 E. 42nd St., New York, N.Y. 10017

ISBN: 0-373-08703-9

First Silhouette Books printing February 1990

Printed in the U.S.A.

DIANA WHITNEY

says she loves "fat babies and warm puppies, mountain streams and Southern California sunshine, camping, hiking and gold prospecting. Not to mention strong, romantic heroes!" She married her own real-life hero fifteen years ago. With his encouragement, she left her longtime career as a municipal finance director and pursued the dream that had haunted her since childhood—writing. To Diana, writing is a joy, the ultimate satisfaction. Reading, too, is her passion, from spine-chilling thrillers to sweeping sagas, but nothing can compare to the magic and wonder of romance.

THE ADVENTURES OF BIFF BARNETT
PRIVATE EYE

Chapter One

He was wild-eyed and wet, so this must be the place.

Shannon Doherty glanced at the work order on her clipboard and tightened her fingers around the handle of her heavy tool case. "Mitch Wheeler?" Her question was merely perfunctory. As he stood in the doorway, splattered and splotched, he wore the familiar, glazed expression of a man with painfully clogged water pipes.

Nodding, Mitch Wheeler's disbelieving gaze traveled the length of her. "You're the plumber?" A giggling, half-dressed toddler squirmed in his arms and Mitch shifted his stance to accommodate the child's restlessness.

So, thought Shannon, this is the famous Mitchell H. Wheeler. She perused the face she'd last seen grinning from the cover of a supermarket tabloid headlined "Biff Barnett Creator Tells All." Since Shannon was more interested in a newspaper's business section than its comics pages, she knew little of the antics of Mitch Wheeler's cartoon hero, Biff Barnett, Private Investigator. The antics of the man himself, however, were widely reported, and few people in the area hadn't heard of Mitch, who was one of the most eligible bachelors in the Los Angeles suburb of Pasadena.

The female on his arm now, however, was considerably younger than the stunning creatures Mitch Wheeler squired publicly.

Shannon smothered a smile as the energetic baby emitted a delighted shriek and stuffed the man's silk tie into her drooling mouth.

"I'm Shannon Doherty," she said. "A-1 Plumbing and Heating."

Ignoring the fate of his neckwear, Mitch continued to stare in apparent bewilderment. He was attractive, Shannon decided. His brown hair was styled in the conservative cut she remembered from newspaper photographs. Those photos, however, hadn't captured the intensity of his eyes— large amber eyes with thick lashes most women would kill for.

Taken individually, Mitch's features were average, and Shannon judged him to be only a few inches taller than herself. But there was nothing average about the overall effect of the man. She had to admit he had a certain charisma.

She wasn't here to evaluate Mitch Wheeler's animal magnetism, though. She was here to do a job and decided to remind him of that fact.

"Perhaps you could direct me to your problem," Shannon suggested.

He pursed his lips skeptically. "You don't look like a plumber."

"Oh?" She arched one eyebrow. "Well, I can assure you that I don't wear this jumpsuit because it's chic, and I don't carry thirty pounds of tools as part of a physical fitness program."

Mitch Wheeler frowned briefly, then scrutinized the plumbing van parked at the curb. Apparently satisfied, he flashed a devastating smile that offered real insight into the secret of his appeal. He'd changed from endearingly boyish to incredibly sexy in the space of a skipped heartbeat.

"Sorry about the third degree," he said. "You'd be surprised how many young ladies have graced this doorstep in disguises more original than yours."

Shannon blinked in surprise, automatically glancing down at her one-piece work uniform. "You think this is a disguise?" What ego! To presume she was some kind of lovestruck groupie simply because she was female.

Before he could reply, a small movement caught Shannon's eye. A solemn-faced girl peeked around the doorframe like a curious, dark-haired kitten. She scanned Shannon casually, then tugged at the man's belt.

"Uncle Mitch," she said somberly. "The hall carpet is all squishy."

"Uncle Mitch" moaned, then stepped away from the door and motioned to Shannon. "Come in, please. I didn't mean to be rude, I just didn't expect the neighborhood plumbing company to be owned by a gorgeous redhead." He offered another practiced-to-perfection smile.

"My father owns the company. I'm on the time clock like everyone else." She saw Mitch's smile fade and knew her tone had been too brusque. That wasn't like her. Shannon was always friendly and polite. There was no tangible reason that this man should set her nerves on edge, but she felt unreasonably perturbed by him.

Mitch's mouth tightened. "I get the message." With two grim strides, Mitch deposited the wriggling toddler into a net playpen and tugged his chewed tie out of her fist.

"Uncum," the baby said, holding her fat arms out and emphasizing the pleading gesture with a series of grunts. Her round face puckered, then lit with pleasure as Mitch handed her a toy.

Turning to the dark-haired girl, Mitch said, "Rachel, honey, keep on eye on Stefie for me, will you?"

"Okay." Huge brown eyes watched thoughtfully.

"It's the upstairs bathroom," Mitch said, leading Shannon toward the carpeted stairway. "The, ah, commode seams to be—"

His words were drowned as a sandy-haired youngster blasted into the room. "Snyder ate the cake," the boy yelped, "and something sticky's boiling all over the stove."

"Oh, no!" Mitch was through the kitchen swing door in two giant leaps. His voice filtered back, a string of unintelligible mutterings followed by a sharp yell and a colorful oath.

Rachel looked at the distraught boy and issued an ominous prediction. "Boy, Dusty, you're in trouble now."

Dusty paled two shades and his freckles stood at attention. Shannon was startled by a high-pitched yelp, then a huge, hairy creature of indeterminate canine origin barreled from the kitchen. A gray cat vaulted from the sofa, spitting and bristling at the intrusion, then shot upstairs like a furry bullet. When the dog skidded behind Dusty as though requesting asylum, Shannon noticed what appeared to be a coat of vanilla frosting globbed on the animal's whiskers.

"Oh, Snyder," Dusty moaned. "Uncle Mitch'll make you stay outside for sure, now."

Synder's tail vibrated gleefully.

When Mitch reappeared in the doorway, his white dress shirt was splotched with a gooey, caramellike substance. He glowered at the dog and then strode to the stairs, mumbling a statement that Shannon interpreted as a request for her to follow.

Dusty was right on her heels. Mitch paused, frowning at the youngster. "You'd better stay downstairs." Dusty looked crestfallen. "You don't want to get in the way, do you?"

"I won't, honest." Dusty seemed stung by the suggestion. "Can't I help? Please?" This plea was directed to Shannon, as though the boy instinctively knew she offered the best chance of acquiescence. "I can hand you tools and everything."

"Well..." Shannon saw Dusty's gray eyes widen hopefully. "Sometimes I do seem to need more than two hands, and since Rachel is busy helping your uncle, perhaps you could be my temporary assistant.''

"Wow!" Triumphant, Dusty shot up the stairs, disappearing into a doorway at the far end of the hall.

Mitch chuckled. "That'll make his entire week. Thanks for being so understanding. You must like children."

"Yes," Shannon said quietly. "I like children." Like children? Shannon tensed. She loved them and had dreamed of having a huge family of her own someday. But simply loving children wasn't enough. Years ago Shannon had been disillusioned by her own parental inadequacies. Time had dulled the sting of failure, but hadn't erased it.

Her unpleasant memories were interrupted as Shannon realized that Mitch was talking to her.

"Pardon me?"

"I said it shows—that you like children." Mitch's eyes darkened to a deep whiskey color and he'd lowered his voice to a soft, silky timbre.

Shannon felt her skin prickle and realized that the man had somehow turned a few nondescript words into a verbal caress. What's more, he'd done it automatically, like an actor giving a familiar performance.

Her throat felt a bit dry under his frankly male appraisal and she mentally shook herself. At thirty, Shannon Doherty had long outgrown the tendency to fall apart when an attractive man showed interest in her. In fact, she had carefully trained herself to do exactly the opposite.

Quickly pulling herself back into character, she straightened her shoulders. "I do believe Rachel was right, Mr. Wheeler."

"Umm?"

"The carpet *is* squishy."

Mitch blinked, then stared down at the oozing plush under his feet. He muttered something, but Shannon ignored him, continuing down the hall and sloshing into the flooded bathroom.

An inch of water covered the floor, a soaked throw rug dripped from the shower rod and the cat's litter box in one corner resembled a sandy square island.

Dusty sat on the edge of the bathtub, grinning. "Stefie flushed her coveralls," he chirped, obviously thrilled to be the bearer of such news. "Then the toilet threw up."

"I see." Shannon slanted an amused glance toward Mitch, who appeared positively morose. "I assume that's the reason for the baby's immodest attire. How old is she?"

"Fourteen months," Mitch said. "And she hates clothes. That's bad enough, but now that she's figured out how to get rid of them for good—" He glared at the porcelain fixture and Shannon offered a sympathetic nod.

"No problem," she assured him. "Since diapers were invented, plumbers have made a good living." She set the tool case onto the flooded floor. "I'm sure that coverall retrieval follows the same basic recovery principles."

"That's reassuring." Mitch looked uncomfortable. "Uh...as long as you're here..." His voice trailed off and he cleared his throat.

"Yes?" Shannon paused, looking up politely.

"The, uh, shower leaks and I wondered... If your schedule allows, of course—"

"I'll be happy to have a look at it."

Mitch offered a strained smile and Shannon had the distinct feeling that he had something besides dripping showerheads on his mind. He continued to stand in the doorway as if he had words stuck in his throat and was about to choke on them.

"Is there anything else, Mr. Wheeler, or shall I begin?"

"Oh, no. Nothing else. You go right ahead and get started," he said awkwardly. "I'll be downstairs if you need me." He backed into the hallway and disappeared.

Shannon turned to Dusty. "Now, Mr. Temporary Assistant, we have work to do."

Dusty beamed.

* * *

In less than an hour, the primary emergency had been resolved.

Dusty, Shannon had discovered, was a verbal encyclopedia of information on Wheeler clan history and seemed delighted to have a captive audience. She'd learned that he was seven and his sister, Rachel, was five and Uncle Mitch had come to live with them before Halloween, which was about six months ago. The youngster obviously adored his Uncle Mitch, and since several of the boy's ideas had been turned into Biff Barnett plot lines, Dusty took personal credit for the success of Mitch's syndicated cartoon strip.

The household itself seemed to be in total chaos—a delightful contrast to the silence of her own childhood environment. A constant cacophony of door slams, dog barks and human noise reverberated throughout the vintage frame house.

As Shannon rewound the heavy toilet auger, Dusty was reciting his experience as flag bearer in last year's Cub Scout honor ceremony.

"Then Dad said he'd pay for the light bulbs and Mom told me it wasn't my fault that the ceiling was too low."

Shannon chuckled and tucked the coiled metal into the toolbox. "Your parents sound like my kind of people."

"Yeah. They're neat." Dusty's voice had lost some of its enthusiasm, and something in his tone—something sad and wistful—caught Shannon's attention. His small finger outlined the shape of a crescent wrench as he added, "They're not here now."

"Oh?"

"They're skiing."

"That sounds like fun. I heard that Mammoth had a spring snow last week. Is that where they went?"

Dusty's shoulders rotated in a listless shrug. "Maybe. They've been gone a long time." He fidgeted quietly for a moment and when he spoke again, Shannon knew he was fighting tears. "Uncle Mitch says they won't ever come back. He said they had an accident and that they d-died."

He stood up quickly, wiped at his face and lifted his chin. "But I don't believe him. My mom and dad would never leave us. Never."

Shannon was stunned to realize that these three beautiful youngsters were orphans.

It wasn't fair. It just wasn't fair.

A lump wedged in her throat. It was a painful déjà vu of Shannon's own childhood. She understood Dusty's denial, his feelings of abandonment, of suppressed fury. She gently brushed Dusty's pale, trembling cheek, then she sat on the edge of the tub and pulled the boy beside her.

"I'm so sorry," she whispered. "I know how much you must miss them, how much it hurts."

"You don't know." His voice cracked. "Nobody does."

"I'll bet you feel angry at them for leaving you." Shannon saw Dusty's surprised expression. "May I tell you a story?"

"I don't care," he said with a shrug.

"When I was about your age, my mother and father decided to have another baby. I was so excited. I wanted a little brother or sister more than anything in the world."

Dusty sniffed. "That's dumb. Sisters are a pain."

"Ah, but I was so lonely, you see. All my friends had big families and I wanted a big family, too. When my mother went to the hospital, she told me she'd be back in two days and she'd bring our new baby."

In spite of himself, Dusty's interest was piqued. "Did you get a brother?" he asked hopefully.

She shook her head. "No, Dusty. My mother never came back. She died and so did my baby sister."

Dusty's chin stiffened. "She must not have loved you any more."

It was the reaction Shannon had expected and she slipped her arm around his small shoulders.

"That's exactly what I thought at the time. I was so angry at her for leaving me." Shannon had to pause and clear her throat. "In fact, I was mad at everybody. I blamed my father for taking her to the hospital and I even blamed myself for wanting a brother or sister.'' Dusty's face had become blurry. Shannon blinked to clear her vision and wondered what had possessed her to dredge up such painful memories. Then she felt the telltale quiver under her arm and knew.

"It wasn't your fault," Dusty said. "You couldn't help it."

"I know that now, but I didn't then. I wasn't as big as you are or as smart. My mother didn't want to leave me, and your parents didn't want to leave you. I'm sure they loved you very much."

Dusty considered this. "Did you cry?"

"Yes, I cried."

"Did you ever stop missing her?"

"No. I think of her every day. Good thoughts, good memories." She sniffed, discreetly dabbed at her eyes, then forced a cheerful voice. "Now, little man, we still have a shower to fix. How would you like to take this water vacuum out to my truck while I have a look at the shower head?"

Dusty hiccuped and stood up. "Okay. Then can I help some more?"

"Of course." Shannon smiled, pushed a tousled thatch of hair from his forehead. Something caught her attention and she turned to stare directly into Mitch Wheeler's somber face.

Oh, Lord. How long had he been standing in the doorway? Shannon wondered. His grim expression told her he'd been there long enough.

A split second later, Dusty saw him. "The toilet's all fixed," he said with renewed enthusiasm. "I helped."

Mitch's smile seemed sad. "That's great, sport, but it's time for you to get cleaned up."

"Aw, we're not done yet."

"I know, but it's getting late." At Dusty's bleak expression, Mitch turned to Shannon. "How much longer?"

"Half an hour." Her gaze fell on Dusty. "Maybe longer, without my helper."

Dusty glowed at the praise.

Mitch relented. "All right, but in thirty minutes I want you changed and scrubbed."

Nodding enthusiastically, Dusty agreed and with a smile of indulgence, Mitch turned to leave. When he glanced back, his eyes locked with Shannon's and she felt pinned by his penetrating gaze. She tried to identify the combination of emotions in his expression. Was it sadness, gratitude, fear? Then it changed and she felt her skin warm. There was no doubt about the message in his eyes now: it was a promise.

Then the doorway was empty.

Dusty took the water vacuum out to Shannon's truck while she dismantled the recalcitrant shower head. As she'd suspected, a new gasket would resolve the problem nicely.

When Dusty returned, she had just located the proper size. "What can I do now?" Dusty grinned expectantly.

"Well, as soon as I get this put back together, you can turn the water on for me and we'll test the gasket." She saw confusion in the boy's eyes and pointed under the sink. "See that silver knob? That controls the water from the main line to this room. When I tell you to, you turn it all the way to the right, okay?"

"Okay." Scrunching down, he ducked his head under the sink and grabbed hold of the knob in question.

Shannon repositioned herself under the shower and began her work. She heard Dusty's voice, kind of a muffled question that she couldn't quite catch. "Umm? What did you— No!" Water exploded from the pipe over her head. "Turn it off, Dusty!"

Dusty finally got the message, but not before Shannon was wet enough to look as if she had just swum the English Channel. The boy's eyes widened in shock as he began to stammer an apology.

"It's all right," she told him, not at all certain she meant it. She gratefully accepted the towel he offered.

"I thought you said to..." His voice trailed off in a childish moan.

"Don't worry, I won't melt." She wrapped the towel around her head and rubbed her shoulder-length hair. Ineffectually, she dabbed at the drenched cotton overalls hanging from her shoulders like a lead weight. Swell.

"I can fix it," Dusty promised, rushing from the room. He reappeared with a blue velour bathrobe. "I'll put your uniform in the dryer."

She took the robe reluctantly, eyeing the monogram—MHW. Not much doubt as to whom the robe belonged to. A distinctive male scent wafted from the fabric. It was vaguely disturbing.

"Ah, I don't know."

"It'll be dry by the time you're done, honest."

He looked so pathetic. Besides, he was probably right. She still had to reassemble the fixture and if she drove back to the office like this, the cloth van seats would be soaked to the springs.

Oh, what the heck.

Dusty headed out the door and the exchange was made. As Shannon finished her work, she found herself straining to hear the muffled giggles and conversations from downstairs. Soon she was humming, feeling more contented than she had in years. If noise was the measure of a happy home, she decided, this house was ecstatic.

After the shower repair had been completed, Dusty still hadn't returned. Not one to sit idly, Shannon dug into her toolbox and retrieved a textbook. She frequently snatched study time during the day. It seemed the only way to compress her busy schedule into a mere twenty-four hours.

From the toolbox tray, she pulled out a package of slightly squashed Twinkies, consoling herself that, since she had school tonight, this would probably be dinner. Besides, junk food was her only major vice and everybody should have at least one. With a contented sigh, she settled back to read.

Forty-five minutes later, her dry clothing still hadn't arrived and the house had become as quiet as a tomb. Shannon wondered if everyone had left, forgetting that she was still here. She opened the door a crack and heard soft, muffled voices. At least she wasn't alone, but it was obvious that her assistant had forgotten his prime directive.

Stepping into the hall, she cleared her throat, and in a loud stage whisper, called Dusty's name.

Mitch Wheeler ran a comb through Rachel's soft brown hair, then fastened it with a pink barrette.

She faced him soberly. "Do I look pretty now?"

"Pumpkin, you always look pretty." He emphasized it with a hug. Satisfied, she smoothed her ruffled dress and walked regally into the den. Mitch watched her and felt as though his heart had been squeezed. They were his brother's children, but he couldn't have loved them more if they were his own.

As far as he was concerned, they *were* his own.

He thought of the scene he'd witnessed earlier. The green-eyed lady plumber had more going for her than striking beauty, he acknowledged. She was sensitive and special. She'd known instinctively what to say to Dusty—something he himself had been struggling with since the children's parents had died six months ago. Dusty wouldn't accept their death, and Mitch had been at a loss, unable to deal with either the boy's anger or his fantasy that his parents would return to him some day.

Yet Shannon Doherty had seemed to understand. In a quiet, subtle way, she'd shown Dusty, and Mitch himself, that such feelings were normal. It had choked Mitch up to realize that Dusty actually understood that his parents were gone, but had been unable to cope with his feelings of abandonment. Shannon had helped him express that.

Yes, this was one lady Mitch had every intention of getting to know better. Unfortunately it would have to wait. Tonight would require all his attention.

"Uncle Mitch?"

"Umm?" Mitch blinked at Dusty.

"I'm all ready now, just like I promised. When are Grandma and Grandpa coming?"

He glanced at his watch. "In about an hour—" Mitch moaned when his words were interrupted by the doorbell. "Scratch that. They're here."

"Yea-a-a-ah." Dusty darted to the front door, yanked it open and was immediately swept into a perfumed embrace.

There was a flurry of hugs and kisses, everyone talking at once as several months' worth of news was shared simultaneously. Mitch stood stiffly, with a rigid smile pasted on his face as the children glowed with excitement and unwrapped gifts from their grandparents. This was followed by another round of hugs, thank-yous and giggles.

Finally Ruth Gilbert looked at Mitch as though he'd just materialized in front of her. "Hello, Mitch." Her voice was cautious and formal. "It's nice to see you again." She offered her cheek for Mitch's perfunctory kiss.

"It's good to see you, too, Ruth." Then Mitch extended his hand to the handsome, gray-haired man beside her. "Steven. How was your flight?"

"Fine, just fine." Steven Gilbert's greeting was warmer than his wife's, but still somewhat tepid. "This California weather is a marvel. There's still snow on the ground in Boston and it's colder than the devil."

Mitch's strained voice broke the awkward silence. "Well, why don't we go into the living room." He'd been dreading this evening for weeks, ever since he'd received a letter from the Gilberts' lawyer.

"Where's the baby?" Ruth asked.

"She's taking a late nap," Mitch replied. "Otherwise, she'd fall asleep before dinner."

"Oh." Ruth seemed disappointed but followed Mitch into the living room and perched delicately on the edge of the sofa. Steven Gilbert dropped beside her and made room for Rachel, who'd scrambled onto his lap.

For the next twenty minutes, Mitch watched the children with their grandparents and wondered if he was doing the right thing. Was it selfish to want the kids to stay with him? After caring for his nieces and nephew for six months, Mitch couldn't imagine living without them. Besides, he'd prom-

ised Rachel and Dusty that he would never leave them; and
it was a promise he intended to keep, no matter what the
cost.

Too soon it was time for the children to quietly watch
television in the den while the adults discussed issues. Big
issues.

"They look well," Ruth said nervously, "and they seem
quite happy."

"They are." Mitch was adamant.

Steven cleared his throat. "You've done a fine job, Mitch.
No one's trying to say that you haven't. It's just that,
well—"

Ruth interrupted. "Children need a stable home."

"They've got one." Damn. His voice was too harsh, too
defensive, Mitch realized. He forced a smile. "Their wel-
fare is my primary concern."

"Yes, yes. I'm sure it is." Ruth gestured helplessly. "But
as a single man, your life-style is somewhat different than
what they're used to."

Mitch stared silently, then made a decision. "Let's get it
out in the open. You're here because my publicist is doing
too good a job." He saw Ruth's jaw clamp and Steven's eyes
drop. "I can understand your concern, but I assure you that
it's unwarranted. If I lived the kind of life the tabloids de-
scribe, I wouldn't have time to put out a daily cartoon
strip."

Ruth Gilbert laced her thin fingers together and laid them
primly in her lap. "I have no doubt that a certain amount of
distortion is inevitable. However, a certain amount of truth
is also inevitable and that truth makes you unfit to care for
these children."

"Ruth!" Steven Gilbert seemed shocked by his wife's
candor. "That's a bit harsh."

"Perhaps. But it's true." She took a deep breath.
"Mitchell, you know it's nothing personal. We've always
liked you and we were, uh, pleased when our daughter
married into the Wheeler family. But now that—" Her voice

broke. "Now that Donna and Kevin are gone, we must all consider what's best for the children."

Mitch kept his tone calm. "I believe it's best for them to remain in the only home they've ever known."

"Not if they must share it with a womanizer who spends his evenings at Spago's and his nights God knows where." Ruth shook off her husband's restraining hand. "And look at that cartoon strip of yours. It's degrading, it's sexist, it's—it's—"

"It's not me," Mitch said softly. "Biff Barnett is a buffoon—the sort of guy who's always tripping over life and making people laugh. *I'm* not a cartoon character." He stretched his hands out in a pleading gesture. "As for the publicity, all I want is to give you my side of the story. Will you at least listen?"

Dabbing at her eyes, Ruth turned toward her husband. Mitch saw Steven squeeze his wife's arm.

"We'll listen," Steven Gilbert said. "And we'll try to understand."

So Mitch opened his heart and shared it. He knew he had to convince the Gilberts that he wasn't the role model for his carousing cartoon character. Mitch loved the children desperately, and although he knew their grandparents loved them too, he believed it imperative that the kids stay in their own home surrounded by their own friends.

To lose not only their parents, but everything familiar to them—as would happen if they were whisked to Boston—could be irreparably destructive. Mitch explained this to the Gilberts, adding that Dusty was having trouble dealing with his loss and a child psychologist was working with both of the older children.

When Mitch finished, he made his final plea. "Just give me another year before you make a decision to ask for custody. Please. Give me a chance to prove myself to you."

"Well..." Ruth was weakening.

Mitch took advantage and used his perfect smile. "You'll see that the irresistible Don Juan image is merely a figment of my publicist's imagination."

"Certainly it couldn't hurt to give the man a bit of time," Steven urged. "After all, this is the children's home."

"I suppose." Ruth Gilbert seemed defeated.

Steven wiped his brow and emitted a low sigh. "Now that we've got all that settled, how about dinner? I'm absolutely starv—" The unfinished sentence hung in the air as a husky voice filtered into the room.

"Dusty? Du-u-u-usty."

Steven's eyes widened in shock. "Who is that?"

Mitch moaned, then forced a plastic smile. "Ah, just the plumber."

"I beg your pardon?" Steven's eyebrow nearly lifted into his scalp.

Leaping to his feet, Mitch tugged at his collar. "I'll be right back," he mumbled.

Ruth stood. "Perhaps we could just look in on the baby."

"No!" Backing toward the stairs, Mitch straightened both arms as though trying to stop a speeding truck. "I mean, I'm sure the baby's still asleep."

Startled, Ruth said, "I just want a little peek."

"She's a very light sleeper." Mitch cleared three steps in one stride, then glanced over his shoulder to see Ruth and Steven following right behind him.

"Nonsense," Ruth muttered. "I'll be quiet as a—" Then she gasped and her hand flew to her throat.

"Good Lord!" Steven exclaimed.

The Gilberts gazed past Mitch with dual expressions of disbelief.

Following their dazed stares, Mitch had to steady himself. Peering out of the hall bathroom was a beautiful, wet-haired redhead wearing Mitch's bathrobe and a horrified expression.

Chapter Two

Mitch emitted a small croaking sound. Shannon's eyes widened in shock, then her head disappeared and the bathroom door slammed.

Turning, Mitch winced at Ruth's thin-lipped expression. This was a complication Mitch really didn't need. Clearing his throat, Mitch gestured toward the other end of the hall. "That's Stefie's room. Ah, excuse me."

Mitch walked stiffly to the bathroom door, painfully aware that the Gilberts were standing at the top of the stairs as though they'd grown roots. He offered a pained smile, then rapped on the door. "Ms. Doherty? Is there, er, a problem?"

"Go away," came the muffled reply.

Mitch's collar was suddenly too tight. Go away? This was *his* house, for crying out loud. Twisting the doorknob, Mitch pulled the door open, only to have it yanked shut from the other side.

"Please," she pleaded pitifully. "Go away and send Dusty."

Dusty? Mitch frowned. What on earth does Dusty have to do with all this?

Slanting a glance at the stone-faced Gilberts, Mitch forced a bright grin. "The door seems to be stuck." To emphasize how amusing the situation was, he tried a casual laugh. It sounded like a choked gurgle. Trying to appear totally nonchalant, Mitch leaned into the door, forced it open and quickly stepped inside.

Shannon stood in the middle of the room, arms folded across her chest to hold the short robe together. She regarded Mitch sullenly.

Shocked, Mitch allowed his gaze to travel the length of her, then shut the door behind him and he silently berated himself for having removed the lock.

"What—" Mitch swallowed hard. "What's going on here?"

Clutching the robe lapels, Shannon's eyes darted as though seeking an escape route. "I'm waiting for Dusty."

Mitch opened his mouth, but his words turned into a grunt as the bathroom door suddenly flew open and smacked into his back. Lurching forward, he grabbed for the sink but tripped over the toolbox and found himself clutching Shannon instead.

Gasping, she pushed frantically at his shoulders, but his momentum bounced them both off the back wall and they slid to the floor in a tangled heap.

Winded by the impact, Shannon shoved a strand of damp hair from her face and tried to suck air into her lungs. Then she saw the two people standing in the narrow doorway, their mouths gaping, looking as shocked as if they had just stumbled into a Roman orgy. A stylish woman with impeccable silver hair regarded Shannon with rigid indignation. Her gaze dropped and Shannon realized that the robe was bunched halfway up her thighs.

Face flaming, Shannon tugged at the material, trying to salvage a small shred of dignity.

Mitch, who had pulled himself to his feet, was simultaneously hauling Shannon upward and trying to help her adjust the twisted bathrobe. When she angrily swiped his hand away, he was embarrassed to realize just how personal his assistance had been.

The woman spoke in a voice that could have etched solid steel. "I see we are intruding, Steven."

Jarred from his momentary stupor, Mitch said, "Ms. Doherty was merely, ah, merely—" Merely doing *what*? Mitch wondered, and shifted his bewildered gaze to Shannon.

She picked up his cue. "I was merely waiting for my clothes."

"I should think so," the woman said crisply, then turned to the man standing beside her. "Perhaps we should leave, Steven."

The man nodded slightly. If the older man appeared dazed, Mitch Wheeler seemed to be in shock. Shannon wished the floor would yawn open and swallow her whole.

Suddenly Dusty squeezed into the room, took one look at Shannon's predicament and paled. "I forgot," the boy moaned, obviously upset. "I'll get it right now, Shannon. Honest."

The youngster whirled and disappeared. Mitch's confused gaze swept from Shannon to the Gilberts, then back to Shannon.

"What in the world is going on here?" His inquiry was polite, yet Shannon caught the nervous rasp of his voice.

"I think that's rather obvious," said the older woman. Her lips thinned and the man beside her shuffled awkwardly.

Mitch sighed. "Ruth, it's nothing of the sort." He spoke with exaggerated patience. "This young woman is the plumber."

"Oh, for heaven's sake," Ruth snapped. "With all of your faults, I never took you to be a liar, Mitch Wheeler."

Mitch went rigid. "I repeat, Ruth, she is the plumber and I strongly resent—"

The house vibrated under the rapid-fire impact of feet on the stairs, then Dusty pushed his way into the room. "It's all dry," he said, panting, and thrust a pile of fluff-dried blue cloth into Shannon's arms. Then he grinned. "I told you I could fix it for you."

Shannon folded her arms around the warm, wadded uniform. "You certainly did, Dusty. Thank you." She turned her attention to the three adults. "If you'll excuse me—"

"Not so fast."

Shannon stiffened at Mitch's sharp tone. "I beg your pardon?"

Ignoring Shannon's indignant gasp, Mitch grabbed the uniform from her arms. He shook it out, holding it to display the embroidered A-1 Plumbing and Heating logo to his guests, then turned to Dusty. "What happened, young man?"

Dusty stared at his own shuffling feet.

Shannon suddenly felt very sorry for the forlorn-looking child. "It was just an accident," she said. "Dusty was helping me with the shower repair and mistakenly turned on the water. He offered to put my clothes in the dryer. And that's all there is to it."

With a triumphant crow, Mitch turned toward the couple still standing as though glued in the doorway. "There, you see? You're always determined to believe the worst of me, aren't you, Ruth."

Ruth sniffed in a haughty gesture. Steven was staring at Shannon with bright eyes and straightening his tie. He stepped forward and introduced himself, allowing Mitch to complete the belated formality. When Shannon realized that she'd just greeted the children's Bostonian grandparents, she stifled a moan. Dusty had mentioned them earlier. What was it he'd said? Something about his grandma not liking Uncle Mitch and wanting to take the children back East. Shannon's heart sank.

Swell. Welcome to California.

Somehow, Shannon managed a plastic smile and nodded when appropriate. After the room had been cleared, she closed the bathroom door, stepped over her tool case and sat shakily on the edge of the tub.

How humiliating! Her mind reran the scene like a speeded-up filmstrip. It was obvious that Ruth Gilbert was unconvinced by the explanation of Shannon's attire.

Pushing aside a guilty twinge, Shannon dressed quickly, ran her fingers through her damp strands of hair and grabbed her toolbox. This simply wasn't her problem, she reminded herself. Mitch Wheeler made his own reputation and now he would simply have to deal with the results.

Mentally reinforcing this thought, Shannon went downstairs.

Mitch was pacing across the entryway. The living room was empty. Looking up, he said, "They suddenly remembered other plans." His attempt to smile fell flat.

"I'm sorry."

"It's not your fault. Ruth's always been a bit pompous and judgmental. She was shattered when her only child married and moved clear across the country." He brightened. "The evening's not a total loss, though—or it won't be if you'll have dinner with us."

"That's very kind of you, but I can't."

"Oh? Is Mr. Doherty expecting you home?" Mitch's expression was totally innocent but his gaze shifted to her left hand. No wedding ring.

In spite of her discomfort, Shannon smiled at Mitch's obvious curiosity, but simply said "No." She stepped around Mitch and walked toward the door.

With a swiveling movement that would have shamed a quarterback, Mitch was suddenly in front of her again, opening the front door.

"No, he's not expecting you? Or no, there's not a Mr. Doherty?" What incredible eyes, Mitch thought. Pale green, like fine jade.

"There most certainly is a Mr. Doherty." Shannon noted Mitch's disappointed expression. She let him digest the information for a moment before adding, "He's my father."

Mitch brightened immediately. "Then how about that dinner? It'd be a shame to let a homemade gourmet meal go to waste." When Shannon shook her head, Mitch added, "I'm a wonderful cook."

"I'm sure you are, but I have school tonight and I'm due in class in less than two hours."

"School?" Mitch looked perplexed.

"Yes. I'm working on a degree in business administration at UCLA."

"I'm impressed. How do you manage all that and still work full-time?"

"I prefer to keep busy. Besides, I only have classes three nights a week."

"Including tomorrow?"

"No, only Monday through Wednesday, but . . ."

"Then tomorrow night, please." His voice and expression had suddenly become serious and got Shannon's attention. "I . . . I need your help," he told her.

"The Gilberts?" The sinking feeling in her stomach intensified.

"Yes."

"What can I do?"

"We'll discuss it tomorrow night." Mitch smiled reassuringly. "The children will enjoy seeing you again. You've made quite a fan of Dusty."

Shannon sighed. The last thing in the world she needed right now was another complication in her life. And Mitch Wheeler was very definitely a complication. For the past few years, she'd stayed away from relationships in general, and when children were involved, such entanglements were to be avoided like the plague.

Still, she did feel some responsibility in this matter.

"All right," she relented. "Tomorrow night, but only to discuss how I can help resolve the problem."

"Of course," he said, with a flash of white teeth. "What else?"

Hmm, Shannon thought, remembering the tabloid headlines. What else indeed?

Still, she took a detour on the way home, pulled up to the nearest newsstand, then thumbed through the newspaper until she found the comics page. "All right now, Mr. Wheeler. Let's just see what you're all about."

THE ADVENTURES OF BIFF BARNETT, PRIVATE INVESTIGATOR

Biff and Police Lieutenant Margaret Kramer face off in Biff's dingy office. Leaning back in his chair, Biff rests his feet on his desk and says, "So one of Willie the Weasel's small-time hoods turned snitch and the mob snatched him. Whaddya want me to do about it?"

Arms folded, Lieutenant Kramer glares at Biff. "Rollo isn't a hood. He's a bookkeeper and an important government witness. Find him."

"I need another case like a shark needs dentures, Maggie," Biff grumbles. "Give me one good reason why I should spin my wheels on this one."

"Rollo's testimony will pull the heart out of the mob and you know more about the Weasel's MO than anyone." Maggie reaches for the doorknob. "And there are two more reasons."

The open door reveals two tiny, sad-eyed children. "If something happens to Rollo they'll be orphans," Maggie says.

Biff gulps.

A tear slides down the smallest child's cheek and Biff groans. "No fair, Maggie. You know I'm a sucker for kids."

Maggie smiles.

It was a typically bright Los Angeles morning. Shannon leaned back in her battered swivel chair, sipping her coffee. The chatter of Lindsay Prescott, receptionist, secretary and disgustingly cheerful best friend, flitted around Shannon's foggy brain like a swarm of humming gnats.

Peeking over the rim of her coffee mug, Shannon smiled in spite of her grumpy mood. Only Lindsay could get away with a wacky outfit like that. She wore a fringed leather vest, matching high-top moccasins and an ankle-length skirt splashed with vivid purple flowers.

Lindsay was leaning against the doorframe. "So it was really him? *The* Mitch Wheeler in person?" Lindsay glided across Shannon's small office like a prima ballerina, pirouetted once, then sat on the corner of the desk and grinned. "Is he absolutely gorgeous? I saw him on the Johnny Carson show once." Lindsay's lean face puckered. "He seemed kind of short, though. I like tall men."

Not surprising, since Lindsay herself was a mere two inches shy of the six-foot mark. At five-foot-eight, Shannon was no munchkin herself, but Lindsay's reed-thin frame was a stark contrast to Shannon's lushly rounded figure.

Lindsay grinned. "Come on, kiddo. Tell all."

"Give me a break." Shannon simply wasn't a morning person. "He's just like anyone else." Even as she said the words, she didn't believe them. Mitch Wheeler was definitely *not* like anyone else.

Lindsay wasn't convinced, either. "*Biff Barnett, Private Investigator* is the hottest cartoon strip since Peanuts and Mitch Wheeler created it. Six months ago, you couldn't pick up a newspaper or a magazine without reading about him. Some feminist group even protested because his cartoon character is such a chauvinist, but I haven't seen a thing about him lately."

"He's been busy, I guess. There was a horrible accident last year. Mitch's brother and sister-in-law were killed."

For once, Lindsay was quiet.

Shannon took another sip of coffee. It was cold. Grimacing, she pushed the cup away. "His brother had three small children, and from what I gather, Mitch has been taking care of them full-time."

"Well." Lindsay drummed her red-tipped fingernails against the desktop. "That doesn't sound like the Mitch Wheeler I've heard about."

"I know. Actually, I've never paid too much attention to gossip columns and tabloids. I usually don't even read the comics, so until yesterday I had no idea what this Barnett character was all about.''

Lindsay made an impatient noise. "When have you had time? Between this job, looking after your father—who, by the way, is more than capable of looking after himself—and going to college three nights a week, I'd be surprised if you even knew who's running for president."

Shannon blinked. "Is there a presidential election this year?''

"You see how you are?" Lindsay wriggled her finger reproachfully. "Honestly, Shannon, I worry about you. There's more to life than clogged drains and the Dow Jones Average."

Shannon sighed. She'd heard this speech before. "I like economics and I'm going to need a college degree—"

"To take over the business some day," Lindsay concluded. "I know, I know. But you need to think about yourself and what *you* want. To hell with the business."

"Lindsay!''

With an annoyed flicker of her hand, Lindsay replied, "You know what I mean. Your father built this business from scratch, and it's his entire life." She leaned forward, her voice low and serious. "It doesn't have to be your entire life, Shannon. There's a world out there."

"I've experienced that world. I don't like it."

"You had a raw deal, no doubt about it, but that's over now. Give the world another chance."

"I'm doing just fine," Shannon insisted.

Lindsay said something unladylike.

The customer bell announced someone's entrance into the lobby and Lindsay looked pained. "Nuts. Well, duty calls," she said, then slipped off Shannon's desk and went into the other room.

Shannon loved her best friend dearly, but was grateful to be alone for a few moments. More from habit than interest, she absently flipped through the day's work orders, then impatiently pushed them aside. It irritated her when Lindsay made comments about her father. Lindsay seemed to think that Frank Doherty took advantage of Shannon, but that was a ridiculous notion.

After Shannon's mother had died, Frank had raised his daughter alone. He'd sacrificed without complaint, spent uncountable nights sitting up with her through chicken pox, colds and bouts of flu. He'd comforted her when she was always the last one picked for the class kickball team. He'd loved her no matter what, convincing Shannon that a gangly, carrot-topped ten-year-old would someday evolve into a graceful, red-haired beauty.

If Pop had been a bit overprotective, that was to be expected. After all, Shannon was the only family Frank Doherty had left.

Having rewarded her father first with the usual adolescent rebellion and later by becoming involved in a marriage and a scandalous divorce, Shannon had spent the past six years trying to atone.

"Shannon, look!" A huge vase of red roses swept into the room over Lindsay's legs. "Who are they from? It's not your birthday, is it?"

The flowers sat on the desk inches from Shannon's startled face. A small envelope thrust out of the foliage on plastic prongs. It teased her, daring her to confront the message within. She stared.

Lindsay wasn't so patient. "Open it," she urged, plucking out the envelope and pressing it into Shannon's limp palm. "Please. I'm dying of curiosity."

Shannon's stiff fingers complied. The note was printed in neat capital letters and Shannon found herself smiling at the thought that the message should have been surrounded by a speech bubble, like in the funnies.

"Well?" Lindsay was close to bursting.

"Read it yourself."

The tiny card was snatched away and Lindsay quickly read it. "'Something in red for my lady in blue. See you up at eight. Mitch.' Oh, Lord," she moaned, then slumped into a side chair and glared at Shannon. "Apparently you no longer trust your oldest and dearest friend."

"Don't be absurd, Linnie." Shannon cleared her throat and folded her hands primly. "There's nothing to tell. It's merely, umm, business."

Lindsay frowned. "Monkey business."

"Not at all. I was simply in the wrong place at the wrong time and, ah, caused a bit of a problem for him." She felt a slow heat creep along her cheeks at Lindsay's knowing stare. "You see, I was in the hall waiting for my clothes—"

"Your clothes?"

"Ah, yes, and Mitch came upstairs with this nice-looking couple—"

"Where were your clothes, Shannon?" Lindsay's voice was deceptively cheerful.

"In the dryer. I was fixing the shower and I got wet, so—"

"So you strolled nude into the hall?" Lindsay gave a low whistle. "No wonder he's sending you roses."

Shannon clamped her teeth and spoke through them. "Do you want to hear this or not?"

Lindsay immediately leaned across the desk and rested her chin in her hands. She smiled sweetly. "Believe me, I am all ears."

In a stilted voice, Shannon told a fascinated Lindsay the entire story. To her credit, Lindsay kept a straight face, nodding in encouragement, appearing to empathize with Shannon's predicament.

In a final, hurried gush, Shannon finished. "So you can see that this isn't actually a date."

"Of course not." Lindsay made a production of inhaling the heady rose perfume.

Shannon scowled. "I promised I'd do what I could to help resolve the problem. For the children's sake."

Lindsay traced Mitch's name on the card. "'The children's sake,'" she murmured, then smiled brightly. "If you believe that, I've got some swampland you might be interested in."

"Oh, well that tears it." Pushing back her chair, Shannon stood and grabbed the pile of work orders from her desk. "I've got better things to do than sit here listening to a bunch of silly romantic innuendos." Shannon grabbed a clipboard and jammed the papers under its metal holder. "This whole thing was a mistake. I never should have agreed." Two pens and a pencil were shoved into her breast pocket. "After all, I can simply telephone the children's grandparents, or write them a letter." She strode across the office, flipped open the lid of her toolbox and stared inside. "There's no reason in the world for me to see Mitch Wheeler again."

Shannon slanted an expectant glance in her friend's direction. Lindsay was merely watching, unperturbed, with that maddening, lazy smile tugging at her mouth.

"Well?" Shannon demanded.

Lindsay stretched like a cat, then fluffed her thick blond curls. "Well, what?"

"I know what you're thinking, Lindsay Prescott." Shannon tossed a variety of tools into the case. "You're thinking that I should go, that I have a responsibility to help if I can."

"I am?"

"Well, I'm not going to do it." There was a loud snap as the toolbox was closed and locked. "I've learned my lesson, especially about men with children."

"That was a long time ago, Shannon. Let it rest."

"Let it rest?" Shannon's voice was suddenly soft, sad. "Okay, sure. After all, the marriage only lasted a couple of years, ruined my reputation and broke my father's heart."

Lindsay was across the room in a flash. "Look, Shannon, your stepdaughter was spoiled and scared. She wouldn't have accepted any woman who shared her precious daddy. None of it was your fault."

Shannon felt her muscles relax. "I know you're right, Linnie. It's just that there's something about Mitch Wheeler that bothers me." She felt a bit sheepish.

"Umm." Lindsay's chin jutted as she propped her glasses on her nose and gave an excellent imitation of a Freudian psychiatrist. "This man is attractive and you—how you say?—are having the physical response to him, no?"

In spite of herself, Shannon laughed. Lindsay was irreverent and occasionally blunt, but she always put things in perspective. "He's very attractive and I'm having a response to him, yes."

Lindsay straightened and dropped her glasses. They dangled at her chest by two cords. "So there you are. Come on, Shannon, you don't have to marry the guy, but it's the first time in years that you've even looked twice at a man."

Still smiling, Shannon shook her head. "No. I don't have time for a relationship."

"Make time." Lindsay's elbow nudged Shannon. "A fling might put a bit of bloom in those cheeks. Celibacy is fine, up to a point—or so they tell me."

Shannon hoisted the tool case and tucked her clipboard beneath her arm. "I'm not going." She walked to the door, angling a glance over her shoulder. "And that, my wily, romantic friend, is that."

An ungodly sound was emanating from the Wheeler house. Shannon paused on the doorstep wondering who, or what, was being tortured inside. Squawk after muffled squawk filtered through the closed front door and for the fifth time in the past two hours, Shannon wondered why she couldn't simply have picked up the phone and given Mitch Wheeler a resounding "Thanks, but no thanks."

It wasn't too late, she told herself. She could turn around right now and disappear into the night. Yes, that's exactly what she would do.

Her own traitorous finger reached out to ring the doorbell.

Shannon moaned. It was too late now. She could hear the soft patter of scurrying feet coming closer, ever closer to the door. Suddenly light flooded the porch and the muffled squeals became louder.

"Hi." Rachel's small dark head tipped back to scrutinize Shannon. "Uncle Mitch said you were coming."

"Hello, Rachel." Shannon's smile was genuine. Rachel was a lovely child, with liquid fudge eyes that seemed to hold the wisdom of ages. Such a solemn little girl, Shannon thought, as though a wizened old sage had been captured in a five-year-old body and clothed in footed Minnie Mouse pajamas.

Rachel motioned politely and Shannon stepped into the tiled entry. The child said something to Shannon at the same moment that a nerve-splitting screech vibrated the room.

"Good grief!" Shannon stared at a closed door at the far end of the entryway. The noise seemed to originate behind that door. "What on earth is that horrible howling?"

"That's Uncle Mitch," Rachel said. "He's playing his oboe."

"You mean he's doing that on purpose?"

Rachel nodded. "He says it relaxes him, but he only does it when he's worried about something."

"What is he worried about?"

Rachel grimaced and shrugged childishly. "I dunno, but he started right after Grandma called."

"I see." Shannon wondered if that call had anything to do with last night and felt a slow anger rising. If the Gilberts were still in a huff over that innocent incident, they must be haughty, self-righteous people. She'd seen enough of those kinds when she was growing up, people who had shunned Shannon because her clothes weren't new enough or stylish enough. People like that frosted Shannon royally.

"I'll get Uncle Mitch," Rachel said, then demurely padded away.

Shannon glanced around. The living room to her right was spacious and sparkling, furnished with rich woods and deep-cushioned comfort. It was inviting, comfortable, smelling faintly of lemon wax and baby powder. She could picture the Sunday papers scattered across the carpet, coloring books on the coffee table and small bodies sprawled happily. But now the playpen was missing and the room was dressed for company.

"Shannon!" Dusty bounded down the stairs.

Shannon smiled at his exuberance, noting that Rachel moved with quiet elegance while Dusty seemed to fly and bounce and skid. "How's my favorite helper?"

"Great," Dusty said, then took a gulp of air. "Grandma and Grandpa Gilbert took us to the zoo today. We saw everything, even tigers and bears and elephants. Then we had hot dogs and cotton candy and Stefie barfed all over the stroller." He grinned up at her, then his eyes widened. "Boy, you look different."

"Well, I don't wear my uniform unless I'm working." Self-conscious, Shannon smoothed the skirt of her apple-green sheath. The dress was her most flattering, with its silken material clinging softly to every curve. She felt her face flame at Dusty's disappointed appraisal.

"Gee," he said sadly. "You look like a girl."

A rich male voice agreed. "She certainly does."

Surprised, Shannon turned to see Mitch watching her with intense interest. His assessment was every bit as thorough as Dusty's had been, but the soft glow in his eyes told Shannon that he, for one, wasn't the least bit disappointed.

Her throat was suddenly dry. She cleared it. "Good evening, Mr. Wheeler."

"Call me Mitch, please." He moved toward her. "I'm so glad you could come."

"It's the least I could do." Her voice sounded prim and stilted. Her words simply sounded stupid. "I mean—" She had no idea what she meant, not while Mitch Wheeler was standing less than a foot away. A spicy-soft scent wafted around her, very stirring, very male, very Mitch. Their eyes seemed to be locked. Such unusual eyes, Shannon thought, the color of rich golden whiskey. His pupils darkened, a sensual communication that he liked what he saw.

"Uncle Mitch?" Dusty's voice was impatient and a bit whiny. "Can I show Shannon my room?"

"Umm?" Mitch seemed reluctant, but finally allowed the spell to break and turned his attention to Dusty. "Not tonight, sport. Shannon and I have some business to discuss. Besides, young man, it's bedtime."

"Aw-w-w-w-w-w..."

"Pronto." Mitch bent to tousle the sandy hair and give the squirming boy a hug. Then he scooped Rachel into his arms and plastered noisy kisses from neck to cheek until she giggled helplessly. "Say good-night to Shannon," Mitch said, and both children dutifully complied. Then he nodded toward the living room: "Make yourself at home. I'll be right back."

Shannon wandered into the sitting room and listened to the sounds of muted laughter and small, running feet above her. She smiled, feeling pleased that Mitch could bring such childish delight from solemn little Rachel. Shannon, too, had been a quiet child. She had no memory of giggles, however, or of being lifted and smothered with kisses, or of noise and laughter in the small house she'd shared with her father.

Shannon could barely remember her mother but sometimes, late at night, she could smell sweet jasmine and hear a soft, familiar lullaby float through the darkness.

It wasn't that Shannon had been unhappy. Frank Doherty was a serious man, hardworking and sometimes withdrawn, but Pop had raised her the best he could. And Shannon loved him for it.

Shannon knew how difficult it was for a man alone to bring up a child. But *three* children? Mitch Wheeler must be unique.

Shannon noticed a group of framed photographs lovingly arranged on a cherry-wood end table. She recognized some of the faces—Rachel as an unsmiling, dark-haired toddler; Dusty with a crooked grin in what appeared to be a school picture; and a bald, wrinkled newborn. Stefie?

There was another photograph—one that tugged at Shannon's heart. It was a family portrait with the three children surrounding a beautiful brunette and a proud-looking man. Shannon noticed a family resemblance. The man looked a lot like Mitch, only younger, perhaps taller.

"It was taken last summer," Mitch said from the doorway. "That's my brother, Kevin, and my sister-in-law, Donna."

"The children's parents?"

"Yes."

Mitch's expression was impassive, but his eyes reflected deep sadness. Shannon turned her gaze back to the photograph in her hands. "They were so young," she murmured. "What happened?"

"It was a skiing accident at Mammoth. Kevin was a good skier but Donna was a beginner. No one is exactly sure what happened, but it appears that Kevin had an accident and Donna tried to go for help. A freak storm hit and . . ." His voice trailed off and he swallowed. Mitch took the picture from Shannon, brushed his fingertips over the glass, then set it back on the table. "The rescue team found them the next day, but it was too late."

"I'm so sorry." Shannon tried to control the stinging in her eyes. They'd had their lives ahead of them, a beautiful family to raise. "It just isn't fair."

"No," Mitch said softly. "Life isn't always fair."

Mitch's response surprised her, then she realized she must have spoken the words out loud. "Was Kevin your only brother?"

Her question drew a light laugh. "I have two other brothers and two sisters. There were six of us." He offered a conspiratorial smile. "I learned how to change diapers as soon as I was out of them myself."

"Goodness! I can't imagine what it would be like to have five brothers and sisters." Shannon tried to picture herself in such a setting. "It must have been chaos," she said. "Are you the oldest?"

"Nope, right in the middle, with all the psychological idiosyncrasies that come with the position." He cocked his head. "Why aren't you married?"

"I beg your pardon?"

"You're a beautiful woman. I can't believe that some man hasn't snapped you up by now."

"What a chauvinistically quaint notion."

"Chauvinistic? Me?" Mitch was genuinely startled by the thought. "Actually, nothing could be further from the truth. I respect a woman's right to pursue a career, I believe in equal pay for equal work and I prefer women with highly developed intellect. I'm a completely liberated, thirty-four-year-old modern man."

"You should mention that to your public relations staff," Shannon advised. "That is definitely *not* the Mitch Wheeler that I've heard about."

He winced. "Touché. My PR man is convinced that any publicity is good publicity as long as they spell my name right. His image-maker ideology has caused me no end of problems."

Shannon regarded him cautiously. "So, will the real Mitch Wheeler please stand up?"

Mitch brightened, and grasping Shannon's elbow, propelled her toward an exquisitely set dining table. "For you, my life is an open book. What do you want to know?"

She met his gaze without blinking. "Why hasn't some woman snapped you up by now?"

Mitch's eyes widened, then he appeared amused that she'd thrown his own trite line back at him. "A few have tried."

"Humility becomes you."

Mitch frowned. "Did that sound conceited?"

"A bit."

"Oh." He cogitated this for a moment. "I really would like to get married someday. You know, the house in the suburbs, kids, dogs, the whole nine yards. My parents had a wonderful relationship and I'm looking for the same kind."

"You've already got the house, the kids and the dog. All you need is the wife."

Mitch laughed. "True enough. I guess the bottom line is that I've never fallen in love. Have you?"

"Have I what? Fallen in love?" Normally Shannon would have implemented her standard defense shield to divert such a personal question, but there was something beguiling about Mitch Wheeler. He was so open, so honest and so sincerely interested, that Shannon found herself answering his questions. "Yes, once. I was very young."

"What happened?"

"I married him." Shannon saw Mitch's stunned expression. "We've been divorced for several years and I took back my maiden name."

"Well." Mitch regarded her thoughtfully. "That explains it."

"Explains what?"

"Why you're so good with children. How many do you have?"

Shannon stiffened. "I have no children." The brisk statement was true, yet it was not true.

Mitch was startled by the harsh tone of her voice. "I'm sorry," he said. "I've upset you."

"Not at all." The words were clipped, false. She was indeed upset and Mitch was quite obviously aware of it.

She'd overreacted again and the painful realization embarrassed her. Mitch had no way of knowing how painful it was to think about Trudy, her stepdaughter. After all these years, the sharp memories had dulled but had not disappeared.

Perhaps they never would.

Chapter Three

Mitch refilled Shannon's wineglass, then settled beside her on the sofa.

"Dinner was delicious," Shannon said. "I love chicken cordon bleu."

Mitch was pleased by the compliment. "It's one of my favorites, too."

"What brand is it?"

"Brand?"

"Yes. I'd like to try it myself." Shannon raised her glass, then realized that Mitch appeared confused by her question. A thought struck her. It seemed impossible, but— "You didn't make that meal from scratch, did you?"

"Of course." Surprise turned to shock. "You didn't think it was one of those frozen atrocities, did you?"

It was Shannon's turn to be shocked. "Of course."

Mitch was insulted. "Now who's being chauvinistic? I'll have you know I've been cooking since I was nine."

Shannon was appropriately chastised. "I'm impressed. The entire meal was fabulous."

"Thank you." Mitch appeared somewhat mollified. "It's not so difficult, actually. Anyone could do it."

"I couldn't." Shannon wasn't being apologetic, simply factual. "If it doesn't come out of a can or a box in the freezer, I don't bother."

"Ugh."

Shannon arched one eyebrow. "I don't do windows, either. I can, however, replumb your entire house, build a new set of kitchen cabinets and, if necessary, tune up the engine of your automobile."

Mitch winced, then managed a smile. "I guess we're even. My plumbing experience is limited to liquid Drano, I couldn't hit a nail straight if you paid me and I haven't the vaguest idea of how to change a spark plug." His grin turned mischievous. "But can you draw?"

"Only stick figures. Can you lay wallpaper?"

"God, no! I wouldn't even try." Mitch chewed his lower lip. "Can you play a musical instrument?"

Shannon stared straight at him and remembered the horrid screech of Mitch's oboe. "No," she answered cautiously.

"Aha!" Mitch gloated. "Neither can I."

Laughing, Shannon silently acknowledged that he had surprised her again. Mitch Wheeler was definitely not what she'd expected. He was charming and funny, arrogant one moment, yet poking fun at himself the next. Mitch was an odd combination of strength and sensitivity; most certainly all man, but with an endearing aura of boyish appeal.

And he was incredibly attractive, but Shannon had yet to isolate exactly how. Mitch was average height. His build was unspectacular—not too lean, yet certainly not overly muscular. His eyes were too round to be considered classically sexy, yet she got goose bumps under his gaze. His lips weren't full enough to be called sensual, yet she found her attention riveted to his mouth.

That mouth seemed to be getting closer.

Alarm bells rang in her brain. She turned abruptly, sipping her wine as she composed herself. Lindsay's opinion notwithstanding, the last thing Shannon needed was a romantic interlude. Brief encounters simply weren't her style, and Shannon's life was much too full for anything as demanding as a serious relationship.

She set her glass on the coffee table. "It's been a lovely evening, Mitch, but we still haven't discussed the, ah, problem." Shannon slid a glance at him and saw his expression cool.

"The Gilberts." His tone was resigned and flat. "There's really nothing you can do, Shannon."

"Dusty said that they'd spent the day with their grandparents." Shannon watched Mitch's face for clues. She saw none and continued. "Rachel mentioned that they'd called you earlier this evening."

Mitch nodded, then finished his wine in a single swallow. "I think they're going to try to get custody of the children."

"Because of me? That's absurd, that's—"

"No, because of me." He raked his hand through his hair. "I'm afraid my publicist has done his job too well. They don't think I'm able to provide a 'suitable environment for the children.'"

"Oh, Mitch." Shannon sat beside him and laid her hand on his arm. "I'm so sorry."

His smile was stilted. "I know the Gilberts love the kids, but they're like strangers to them. I held each one of those children the day they came home from the hospital." He sighed. "I want to do what's right, what's best for them, but it's difficult to know what that is."

Shannon regarded him thoughtfully and wondered what really made Mitch Wheeler tick. He was famous, probably rich, a sought-after celebrity who could travel all over the world and have his pick of beautiful women. Yet he'd chosen to take in three orphaned youngsters and love them as if they were his own.

Suddenly Shannon realized that Mitch was watching her, too, and his eyes were darkening with sensual pleasure. She felt his hand cover hers, saw his mouth moving toward hers.

In spite of her previous mental lecture, Shannon waited, mesmerized.

A warm, friendly kiss, she told herself. A bit of comfort for a man who needed it. Certainly that couldn't hurt, could it? It was, after all, the charitable thing to do. One kiss. One small, sweet kiss.

A muffled giggle echoed from the hallway.

Mitch stiffened. The sound of running feet on the stairs filtered into the room.

Shannon blinked and pulled away, the spell broken. "What was that?" she asked. The answer came from behind the sofa.

"Uncle Mitch," Rachel said. "Stefie woke up."

Shannon turned and peripherally saw Dusty as he disappeared up the stairway. She heard his boyish chuckle, then a door closed quietly.

"Go back to bed, pumpkin," Mitch told Rachel. "If you go to sleep, Stefie will go to sleep, too."

Rachel seemed to consider this. "But she has to go potty."

Shannon stifled a smile. Mitch seemed extremely uncomfortable. "Stefie's at the age when she's, well, learning how to use the facilities," he explained.

Shannon managed a serious expression and nodded.

Mitch cleared his throat. "I'd better just check."

"Of course."

He fidgeted briefly, tried to look pleasant, then stood and headed up the stairs. Rachel regarded Shannon solemnly, then followed her uncle. Whispered conversation upstairs was punctuated by the sounds of movement and delighted, baby-type babbling.

In a few moments, Mitch returned sporting an absolutely devastating smile. "Now, where were we?" With a smooth, practiced motion, Mitch's arm encircled Shannon's waist as he lowered himself to the sofa.

"Uncle Mitch?"

Mitch froze. He spoke through clamped teeth. "What is it, Dusty?"

"I'm thirsty."

"Then get a drink of water," Mitch said impatiently.

"Okay." Dusty trotted, grinning, into the living room and headed toward the kitchen door.

"In the bathroom," Mitch snapped. "There are, as you know, paper cups and a perfectly good supply of water in the bathroom. Upstairs."

Dusty stopped. "Oh." He sneaked a sly glance at Shannon. "Do you want to see my room now?"

Mitch stood and put his hands on his hips. "No, she doesn't. Upstairs, young man."

"Okay." The boy obviously knew Mitch's limits and had apparently decided those limits had been reached. "Night, Shannon."

"Good night, Dusty."

Mitch glared, Dusty mounted the stairs as though a gallows awaited, and soon the house was still.

Actually, Shannon was both disappointed and grateful for the reprieve. Mitch Wheeler seem to have a hypnotic effect on her. She'd spent years dodging advances from hopeful men and not once had she experienced such longing. She'd wanted Mitch to kiss her and knew he would have done just that if Rachel hadn't interrupted. Shannon suspected that one kiss from this man might be dangerous to her emotional health. Nothing about Mitch Wheeler was ordinary, and nothing about Shannon's reaction to him was safe.

"Actually, it's getting late." She clutched her purse like a shield. "I . . . I should be going."

Mitch protested immediately. "But you haven't had dessert. It's a chocolate mousse cake."

"Don't tell me you made *that* yourself."

Mitch grinned smugly.

"Good grief, you're a wonder. What other hidden talents do you possess?"

Shannon was immediately sorry she'd asked. A slow, sexy smile spread across Mitch's face and Shannon flushed. Most redheads blush easily and Shannon was no exception, although it annoyed her immensely. She was not, after all, a naive schoolgirl.

Mitch however, seemed charmed. "You're actually blushing. I love it."

"It's the bane of my existence," Shannon admitted. "In high school, I blushed at fire drills."

She took a sharp breath. Close. He was too darn close. Shannon had managed to get to the entry hall but was now in danger of losing her will to leave.

Mitch's fingertips whispered across her cheek. "I'd like to see you again. Tomorrow?"

"Umm—well—I have plans for tomorrow." Shannon moaned inwardly. She was stumbling over her words and her brain seemed empty, as though all rational intelligence had escaped by seeping out through her ears.

Mitch's beautiful mouth hovered above her, brushed her lips softly, then covered them in a deep kiss that shook Shannon to the soles of her feet. His arms wound around her and she was pressed against his chest, feeling the heat of his body permeate her thin silk dress. The room seemed to spin and Shannon grabbed Mitch's shoulders as though he were the only tangible object in a whirling universe.

The kiss deepened as he coaxed her lips to part, then tasted her with sweet, savoring strokes.

It was magic. Shannon wanted it to go on forever.

"Uncle Mitch?"

They pulled apart like guilty adolescents. Mitch was breathing heavily and Shannon felt as though she might never breathe again.

Rachel stood patiently at the top of the stairs. Mitch stared at her as though she were a small apparition.

Finally, Mitch found his voice. "Rachel, I told you to stay in your bed and go to sleep, didn't I?"

"Yes, Uncle Mitch." Rachel's expression didn't waver.

Exasperated, Mitch's voice raised to a higher pitch. "Then what are you doing up?"

"Stefie's crib is all wet." Huge eyes stared down reproachfully. "I told you she had to go."

Mitch's mouth moved but made no sound. He appeared to be in shock. When his voice returned, he managed a small croak and a helpless shrug.

"You'd better have a look," Shannon said, fighting to control her own amusement.

He nodded sadly and went toward the stairs mumbling something about children themselves being the world's most effective method of birth control.

The telephone receiver felt cool against Mitch's ear, but there was nothing cool about the voice emanating from the other end of the line.

"Good grief, Mitchell! I'm your brother and even *I* have trouble buying this one. The Gilberts find a gorgeous, half-nude woman in your house and you try to pass her off as the plumber? Come on, man."

"Forget the lecture, Ross, and put on your lawyer hat."

Mitch massaged his throbbing temples. Rotten time for a headache, but bad timing seemed to be Mitch's destiny. "It's the truth."

The line was silent for a moment, then Ross Wheeler sighed. "Yes, I believe it is. The entire situation is too ludicrous to be anything else, but it still doesn't help your case one iota."

"I know, I know." Mitch drummed his fingers on the slanted surface of his drafting table. "What's the next stop?"

"The ball's in the Gilberts' court. It's been there all along." Ross sounded tired. "If they decide to go ahead with the custody suit, we'll have to prove that it's in the best interest of the children to remain in familiar surroundings."

"What about financial considerations? I've already established trust funds for their college education and I have more than enough money to—"

"The Gilberts are just as well off as you are, they're the children's natural grandparents and they have the extra added attraction of a stable, thirty-three year marriage."

"Ruth Gilbert is a coldhearted snob." Mitch's temper was wearing thin. Ross was right. A judge would look at the superficial, compare the Gilberts' country-club existence with Mitch's carefree bachelor exploits and close the book. A desperate rasp shook Mitch's voice. "What can I do, Ross? I know Shannon will help if she can."

"Shannon?" Ross sounded confused and annoyed. "Who is Shannon?"

"The lady plumber."

Ross moaned. "For heaven's sake, find a new plumber and don't see her again."

"What?"

"I realize that the children have kept you too busy to maintain your social calendar the past few months, and as it turns out, that's the best thing that could happen in your case."

Mitch's knuckles were whitening as he grasped the receiver and tried to absorb what Ross was telling him. Not see Shannon? An image of her clung to his mind. Mitch saw her holding Dusty as she shared the child's grief, remembered the way his heart had quickened at the sweet taste of her lips.

"You're going too far." Mitch's voice was low. "Shannon Doherty is special. The kids want to see her again. And so do I."

Exasperation clipped Ross's tone. "Damn it, man. To you, they're all special."

"You haven't even met her. Give her a chance."

"That's not the point. She won't be special to the Gilberts' lawyer and he'll tear her reputation to shreds." Ross fought to maintain a reasonable tone. "If you had a long-term relationship already established, I'd be recommending that you make it legal before the court date. Marriage would make you seem more settled, more worthy."

"Worthy?" Mitch was appalled. "You're telling me the judicial system would find me 'more worthy' of custody if I just grabbed some poor woman and married her? What about commitment to the children? What about loving these kids so much that the thought of losing them makes my guts twist? Doesn't that count for anything?''

"Not as much as the psychologist's report, and that's going to be your biggest selling point," Ross said. "The fact that he feels the children would be emotionally wounded by another upheaval in their lives will carry a lot of weight."

Ross's words had the desired effect. Mitch's breathing slowed and his mind cleared. If only his head didn't hurt so much. Be calm, he told himself. Think.

"I can't go through life in constant fear. It's not good for me and it's not good for the children." Mitch waited for Ross's reluctant agreement. "I have to be myself because I don't know how to be anyone else. If that's not good enough for the Gilberts, if that's not good enough for the court, well, I'll just have to cross that bridge when the road narrows."

Ross's voice was heavy. "Why don't you just read a lawbook and represent yourself? You might as well, if you're not going to follow my advice."

"I'll take all of your advice under consideration."

"Fine. But if I were you, I'd stay off the front pages and I'd stay away from the lady plumber."

With Ross's curt goodbye, the line was dead. Mitch stared at the telephone for a moment, then cradled the receiver. His brother meant well and Mitch knew that Ross loved Kevin's children as much as Mitch himself did, but he also knew that Ross had his own set of emotional baggage to deal with.

After the death of their parents, Ross had stepped into the role of protector and father figure for his five siblings. That, coupled with his brother's divorce and subsequent loss of his own children had colored Ross's view, making him overly cynical.

At least Mitch hoped Ross was unduly cautious. Two days ago, Mitch couldn't have cared less if his brother had told him to enter a monastery until the hearing. How could one woman, even a beautiful, red-haired one, have so quickly captured a heart that had been totally free for decades?

Infatuation, Mitch decided. Merely the result of a starving man suddenly tripping into a sumptuous feast. Ross was absolutely right about one thing: the Gilberts didn't need any more ammunition for their case. But then, Ross had also said that a stable relationship would be helpful. Scratch that—a *legal* stable relationship, otherwise known as marriage.

A few months ago, the *M* word would have made Mitch break out in a cold sweat. Now he actually found himself considering marriage as a possibility. A future possibility, of course, but the vision was still there, etched in his mind beside a beautiful redheaded woman.

Good grief, Mitch thought, *I must be going mad.*

He reached for his oboe.

Shannon rapped on her father's kitchen door, then pushed it open. She lugged a basket of freshly laundered linens to the table. "Pop, are you home?" She heard a shuffling noise in the living room. He was home.

Automatically Shannon sorted the laundry into folded stacks, directing her conversation toward the sounds of movement. "I picked up the groceries you wanted. Can you get them out of the car for me?" She paused, listening for an answering grunt. It came. Satisfied, she continued. "Two bags on the front seat. I can't stay long today. I've got to study for an economics test Monday night."

A rangy man appeared in the doorway and yawned. Shannon smiled at him. "Watching *The World of Science* again, Pop? You know those programs always put you to sleep."

Frank Doherty yawned again, rubbed at his thinning gray-gold hair and grinned sheepishly. "I know they do. It's that danged monotone narration that does it."

"Then why do you watch?"

Frank looked surprised. "Why, it's educational."

Shannon laughed. It was a comfortable conversation with a predictable punch line. She knew that her father would head out the back door for the groceries, stopping on the way to slip an arm around her shoulders, kiss her cheek and tell her she looked mighty pretty this morning. It was their weekend routine and they both looked forward to it.

He didn't disappoint her. "You look mighty pretty this morning, baby." A light kiss, a quick squeeze and he was out the back door.

When Frank returned, he set the grocery bags on the counter and began to unload them. "Where's the bananas? You know I need my potassium—what's this? Now, honey, you know I don't like frozen juice."

"The bananas were all soft and spotted and I had a coupon for the juice." Shannon saw her father's face pucker. "If you don't want it, put it back in the bag. I'll take it home."

Frank's lean shoulders rotated in a halfhearted shrug. "I guess it wouldn't hurt to try it." He set the small can in the freezer. "Now, what's all this about not being able to stay?"

"I have to do some extra studying this weekend. I'll take care of the vacuuming and mop the floors, but then I really have to get going."

"That's okay, baby." Frank's sad face said otherwise. "I appreciate your help, but it's really just an excuse to see you."

Shannon laughed. "You see me every day at work," she reminded him.

"That I do, but it's not the same."

"I know, Pop. I look forward to the weekends, too, but this can't be helped."

"I suppose not. Darned if I know why you won't just move back here. Things wouldn't be so hard for you."

"We've been through this before. I need my space and besides, how could you expect me to live with someone who leaves whiskers in the bathroom sink?"

Frank ignored his daughter's teasing and went to the refrigerator to put away a fresh carton of milk. "I thought you usually did your studying on Friday night so we could have more time together on Saturday."

Shannon's fingers seemed to stiffen as she folded a fluffy towel. She didn't want to discuss the reason she hadn't found time to study last night. The towel received her undivided attention.

Frank Doherty cleared his throat. "I called you last night, but you weren't home."

"Umm." Shannon seemed totally engrossed in smoothing a dishcloth.

"I rented a movie tape for us. I thought when you were through studying, we could have popcorn and watch it together. Like we used to." Pause. "I guess you had something else to do, though." A longer pause. "Because you weren't home."

Oh, good grief.

"You're right, I wasn't home. I made other plans."

"Oh. Well, that's nice, I guess. You don't get out much anymore." Frank fidgeted. "Did you and Lindsay go shopping or something?"

"No."

"Oh. Well, it's really not any of my business. You're a grown woman now."

"Yes, I sure am."

"I'm a lucky man to see as much of you as I do. I mean, how many men can say that their daughter is going to follow in their footsteps and take over the family business someday."

The last part of Frank's sentence followed Shannon down the hall as she filled the linen closet. It was ridiculous, she told herself, not to simply inform her father that she'd had dinner with a very nice man. She knew, however, exactly how the conversation would progress from that point. It was something she would prefer to avoid.

Frank's voice floated down the hall. "I saw some flowers in your office yesterday. Roses. The, uh, card was just laying on your desk—not that I was snooping or anything. I was just looking for a work order."

Shannon shoved the last stack of clean sheets into the closet. "All right, all right." She went into the kitchen, poured two cups of coffee and set them on the table. "You're going to be like a dog with a bone, so I'll tell you. I had dinner with Mitch Wheeler last night." Frank's eyes widened and his mouth opened. Shannon held up her hand. "Yes, *the* Mitch Wheeler."

She sipped her coffee, sighed and related the entire story. When she'd finished, her father was staring into his cup as though trying to read the future in a few scattered coffee grounds.

"Do you like him?" he finally asked.

"Yes, I do."

"But he's got kids, honey. You know what trouble kids can cause."

"They're not actually his children. He's their uncle."

"Same thing." Frank's mouth tightened. "Haven't you learned your lesson yet? What's it going to take, anyway?"

A cold knot twisted Shannon's stomach. It had been six years since her marriage to Robert Harold Willis had ended but the trauma remained, the shadow of scandal still darkened her life.

Willis had been a widower twenty years her senior, with a knack for purchasing the right real estate at the right time. If his financial ventures were a bit shadowy and his sources a bit questionable, Shannon had been too naive to notice. He'd pursued her relentlessly, showering Shannon with the attention and affection she'd desperately needed at the time. The fact that he had a beautiful nine-year-old daughter had made everything seem perfect.

It had been like a dream come true. Suddenly, Shannon had what she'd wanted all her life, a real family. She'd cared deeply for Robert and loved her stepdaughter, Trudy, planning to have more children as soon as possible.

But the dream had become a nightmare. Robert didn't want another child.

For nine years, Trudy had been the love of her father's life, spoiled as only the very rich can be. The child had no intention of sharing her father with Shannon and had sabotaged the marriage with lies and childish tantrums. Then the second shoe had dropped. Shannon could still visualize Robert's tightly drawn face as he'd told her that the truth was unimportant: he'd only married her to have a good mother for Trudy and since Shannon obviously couldn't handle that function, the marriage was over.

At first Shannon had blamed her own inexperience for the failed marriage. Although she now realized that there had been nothing she could have done, she still had secret doubts about her ability to be a good mother.

"Do you hear me, Shannon?"

"Umm? What did you say?"

"The kids are bad enough, but this Mitch Wheeler fellow is even more famous than Willis." Frank made an unpleasant sound. "Maybe *infamous* would be a better word, judging by what I've read about him."

"You can't believe everything you read. You, of all people, should realize that."

"And you should realize that the printed word, truth or not, can destroy lives. Lord, Shannon. Have you forgotten?"

Forgotten? She could never forget. Shannon still saw the screaming headlines during the divorce, innuendos about Robert's purported underworld contacts and shady financial deals. There had even been speculation that Shannon was involved.

It had never gone to trial, of course. Lack of evidence. But that didn't stop the press from roiling with malicious accusations.

Shannon felt suddenly exhausted. "No, I haven't forgotten. I remember the newspaper stories and I remember how hurt you were by them." Her shoulders seemed to melt. She slumped forward, resting her head in her palm.

"It's not me I'm worried about, baby." Frank reached across the table to stroke Shannon's head. He tucked a crooked finger under Shannon's chin, urging gently. When she met his gaze, he smiled. "I just don't want anyone to ever hurt you again."

"I know." Tears pricked at her but she forced a strained laugh. "Well, the wedding was scheduled for tomorrow, but I guess I'll call it off."

Frank Doherty's eyes crinkled. He obviously knew Shannon was joking, trying to break the somber mood. "I haven't returned that tape yet. Why don't you stay and we'll have a real nice evening."

"Okay." She took a deep breath. "Do you want me to fix dinner?"

Frank's smile died. "No! I mean, how about some take-out chicken?"

This time, Shannon's laugh was genuine. "Not feeling suicidal today, huh? Chicken will be great."

She thought of Mitch's cordon bleu, of Rachel's round, wise eyes, of Dusty's exuberance, of Stefie's wet giggles. There was no reason to see any of them again, Shannon told herself, surprised to realize how sad that would be. After all, she'd just met them. If she allowed herself to become involved with the Wheeler clan, to become emotionally attached—well, the potential consequences of falling for another packaged deal were too hideous to even consider.

Her father was right, of course. Nothing good ever happened by ignoring the lessons of the past, no matter how painful those lessons might be. One learns from history, or one is doomed to repeat it, goes the old proverb.

Shannon's marriage had been one history lesson she would never forget.

Chapter Four

Shannon closed the frayed ledger and scrubbed at her burning eyes. Done at last. It had taken most of the afternoon, but the A-1 Plumbing books were up-to-date, everything balanced and Shannon herself had not yet gone blind. More important she had only thought of Mitch Wheeler three times today. Maybe it would be a good weekend, after all.

She stretched indulgently, working the kinks from cramped arms and stiff muscles as she pondered how to broach a business problem. Billable hours were dangerously low. Pop was so stubborn. Shannon feared that if they didn't branch into air-conditioning installation and repair, A-1 Plumbing would soon be unable to compete. Expansion was the only option.

Tomorrow was Saturday, the day she and her father always spent together. Shannon decided she would find some way to bring up her concerns.

Looking up, Shannon saw Lindsay standing in the doorway, grinning like a cat with a defeathered canary. Shannon knew her best friend only too well. Behind that smug grin lurked a devious mind.

"All done with your bookkeeping chores, eh, kiddo?" Lindsay fingered the eyeglasses dangling from her neck. "Made any plans for a big weekend?"

"No, just the usual." What was she up to? Shannon wondered.

"The usual, huh, like hitting the books tonight, cleaning your dad's house tomorrow and burying yourself in a good Western novel on Sunday?"

"I'm not deaf, Linnie, you needn't shout. What's this all about, anyway?"

Lindsay shrugged and looked exceptionally pleased with herself. "Just curious. By the way, you've got visitors in the lobby."

"Visitors?" Shannon frowned. "You mean customers? Tell them the office is closed, Linnie. It's almost five-thirty—"

"Not customers. Visitors." Lindsay stepped from the doorway, disappearing into the lobby. Her voice floated back. "She's available now. Go right in."

Shannon heard the scuffling of small feet and felt a quiver of excitement. She would recognize those scuffles anywhere.

"Hi, Shannon." Dusty Wheeler burst into the room with his usual, tornadolike style. "Is this where you work? Gosh, where's your truck? What are these?" He pointed to Shannon's exhibit shelf. "Can I see one?"

"Slow down, partner." Shannon laughed and tousled his sandy hair as she went to the shelf in question. "These are cutaways of various pumps, meters and other devices." She lifted a heavy anodized water meter that had been sheared in half to display the inner workings.

"Wow," Dusty exclaimed, then barraged Shannon with a series of rapid-fire questions.

Shannon wasn't listening. She was looking at Mitch. He stood in the doorway, politely allowing Lindsay to coo over Stefie. Mitch slanted a glance at Shannon and smiled—a shy, endearing kind of smile. It melted her. Had it really been over a week since she'd seen him? Her insides felt mushy.

Stefie chortled as Lindsay tickled her fat neck. "You're just precious. May I hold her?" Lindsay asked, plucking the wriggling toddler from Mitch's arms before he could reply. "Have fun," she said, then disappeared with the baby.

Not seeming to know what to do with his now-empty hands, Mitch jammed them into his pockets. "Hi," he said, then rocked nervously back on his heels. "Nice office."

Her office was a wreck. "Thank you." Shannon noticed the small figure half-hidden behind her uncle. "Hello, Rachel. It's nice to see you again."

Wide eyes watched Shannon intently. "Hello, Ms. Doherty."

"Please call me Shannon, Rachel. All my friends do."

Rachel looked up at Mitch for a validating nod. When she received it, Rachel took a step into the room and asked, "Is this where you work when you're not fixing toilets?"

Mitch moaned, Shannon laughed. "Yes, honey, this is it."

When Rachel went to join Dusty, Shannon and Mitch alternately fidgeted, smiled and pretended to watch the children.

Finally Mitch broke the tense silence. "We were just on our way to get some ice cream and happened to pass by."

"Oh." Shannon rubbed her damp palms over the front of her jumpsuit and wished she'd changed into street clothes before Mitch had arrived. "How nice," she mumbled.

"I thought—that is, we thought you might like to join us." The words rushed like air from a balloon. "For ice cream. At the park."

There should be a law against eyes like his, Shannon thought. Like glowing amber crystals; hypnotic and exciting.

Lessons of the past, her brain whispered. Besides, her life was too full right now. She had her work, her school, her friends, her father. There was no time for anything or anyone else. No time.

"I'm sorry, but—" She was stammering and that embarrassed her. Shannon cleared her throat. "I have other plans."

Lindsay's cheerful voice sang from the lobby. "No, you don't."

Shannon's mouth snapped shut. So that's what the third degree was all about. Lindsay had purposely set her up, and done it loudly enough so that Mitch could hear.

She managed a stretched smile and said, "Thank you, Mitch. I'd love some ice cream."

A look of relief and genuine pleasure lit Mitch's face.

"If you'll just give me a couple of minutes so I can change?"

"Sure, no problem." Mitch stepped back to allow her access to the doorway. "Take your time."

Shannon's gaze fell on Dusty, who was gleefully dismantling a vacuum suction pump. "I'll hurry."

On her way to the ladies' locker room, she managed a halfhearted scowl at Lindsay. It was wasted, however, because Lindsay flashed Shannon a smug look, then buried her face in Stefie's soft tummy.

In record time, Shannon had slipped into the teal-blue knit dress and low-heeled pumps she'd worn this morning. She examined herself in the full-length mirror, chewing nervously on her lower lip. Then she ran a comb through her fiery hair, replaced her gnawed lipstick and headed back through the lobby.

When she heard her father's voice, her heart started to race. This was not a good time for introductions. Actually, as far as Frank Doherty and Mitch Wheeler were concerned, there would never be a good time.

As she peered into her office, the two men were sizing each other up like prize fighters at a weigh-in. Shannon swallowed. Her father *was* overprotective, but since her mother had died, Shannon knew she was the only family Pop had.

It was true that any man who'd shown interest in Shannon had been treated rudely by Frank, but she'd tolerated his behavior because she understood it. Besides, Shannon had never cared much for any of those men and she absolutely hated confrontations.

Mitch, however, seemed up to the challenge. He was telling Frank Doherty in a low but decisive voice, that he had every intention of seeing Shannon as frequently as the lady would allow. The older man's eyes were as cold as blue flint.

Good Lord. Frantic, Shannon backed away from the doorway and threw Lindsay a pleading glance.

Lindsay smiled sweetly. "Frank came in as soon as you left. I introduced them and they took it from there."

"Why didn't you stop this?" Shannon was trying to whisper through tightly clenched teeth. The result was a raspy hiss. "They're in there sniping at each other like a couple of adolescents."

"Yes. Isn't it wonderful?" Lindsay gave Stefie a squeeze and made gurgling noises against the baby's ear.

"Lindsay Prescott, you set this up."

"I did not!" Lindsay was indignant. "You are thirty years old, Shannon Doherty, and your father has kept you under his thumb long enough. If Mitch Wheeler is man enough to bend that thumb a bit, so be it."

"I am not dominated by my father." Aware of the ears lurking beyond the wall, Shannon lowered her voice. "I spend time with Pop because I *want* to, not because I have to."

"Right." Lindsay stood suddenly and thrust the squirming toddler into Shannon's arms. "Well, I've got places to go and things to do. Toodles." With that, Lindsay grabbed her purse and sauntered out the front door.

Shannon was angry. It seemed to her that everyone was suddenly trying to manipulate her life—her father, Mitch Wheeler, even Lindsay. Nuts to them all. Shannon Doherty was nobody's puppet, she decided. She would make her own choices, do what she wanted to do with whomever she chose—period, end of discussion.

And right now, Shannon wanted ice cream.

The breeze was warmer than usual for this time of year. The reddening sky foretold impending twilight, a warning unheeded by scores of people wandering through the park. A perfect spring sunset, Mitch thought.

He watched Shannon scrub sticky chocolate ice cream from Stefie's face and realized that he couldn't remember ever being so nervous about asking a woman for a date. Not that an ice-cream cone in the park would actually qualify as a date, particularly when chaperoned by three observant youngsters, but it was close enough to have Mitch's innards in an uproar.

How many times had he picked up the telephone in the past week, ready to dial Shannon's number only to remember Ross's warning? For six months Mitch hadn't bothered seeking female companionship and hadn't missed it. Now, when any innuendo, when even the vaguest appearance of impropriety could sabotage his chances of retaining custody of the children, Mitch realized that he may just have found the woman of his dreams. He had to see her again—and again and again and again.

Shannon seemed so right with the children. Watching her now, Mitch had to smile. Stefie's little face was furrowed in concentration as Shannon tried to clean one gooey hand.

"I—keeem," Stefie said. "Ickers."

"I know, honey," Shannon said. "Ice cream *is* ickers, especially when you take it out of the cone."

Rachel tugged on Shannon's arm, then pointed toward a drinking fountain across the walkway.

"Good idea, Rachel. Aren't you the clever one!" Shannon scooped Stefie up and headed toward the fountain. Rachel followed, obviously pleased by Shannon's praise.

As Shannon held Stefie's fat hands under the water, Mitch watched with a sense of wonder. Most women dressed in an elegant knit would be appalled at the thought of chocolate ice cream and drooling babies. Shannon, however, had simply taken it in stride.

Mitch's throat tightened. God, she was beautiful. Shannon's face was aglow, framed by thick hair cascading like shining strands of liquid copper. She laughed as Stefie splashed in the watery arc.

No doubt about it, he was totally infatuated. It was a first for Mitch and he was both unnerved and fascinated by the sensation.

Shannon was still laughing as she sat on the bench beside Mitch. She plopped the delighted baby on her lap. "Well, the hands made it, but the shirt didn't." A large chocolate stain smeared the tiny T-shirt that had the words Potty Animal emblazoned on the chest. "Your housekeeper will not be happy."

Mitch issued a disdainful sound. "I don't have a housekeeper."

"Why not? Surely you can afford it. It must be terribly difficult to maintain your career and care for three small children."

"I'll manage." His voice softened. "Besides, the children have a rough enough time of it right now. They don't need some stranger hovering over them."

"I see." Shannon noted that the housekeeper subject was closed and turned her attention back to the stained shirt. "Cold water and a squirt of prewash should fix it."

Mitch eyed the shirt. "I've seen worse."

"I can imagine." Shannon's gaze fell to Dusty. His pale blue corduroy pants sported two thoroughly green knees. "How do you get out grass stains?"

"I don't. When they get too bad, I just iron those patches on them." Mitch feigned an innocent expression. "I'm new at this, remember?"

Her expression was skeptical. "I thought you were raised doing this kind of thing."

"The laundry was my mother's domain. We just tossed our clothes in the hamper and stood back." Mitch slid her a glance. "Sounds like laundry is your specialty, as well."

"Why do you say that?"

"Well, you know how to get chocolate out of a T-shirt, and I thought I heard your friend say that you do your father's laundry." Mitch saw Shannon's expression tighten and knew he'd moved into a delicate area. It had been deliberate. He'd been at first surprised, then annoyed at her father's reaction to him and had hoped that Shannon would volunteer some insight into that behavior. When she didn't comment, Mitch tried the direct approach. "What has your father got against me, Shannon?"

She tensed. "Nothing, really."

"Then why would he say 'My daughter's got no time for the likes of you'? That's not exactly what I expected to follow a perfectly civil introduction."

Shannon winced. "He said that? I'm sorry, Mitch. I guess Pop tends to be a bit, ah, overprotective."

That was an understatement, Mitch thought. The man had been downright hostile. "Why? I mean, you're a grown woman, and a very beautiful one. I felt as though I was escorting a fifteen-year-old to the prom."

Shannon set Stefie on the grass. She was obviously uncomfortable and Mitch had a fleeting urge to change the subject. The urge passed. Something was going on here, Mitch told himself—something that affected Shannon very deeply. He sat quietly, watching her, waiting patiently for her to speak.

Finally, she did. "I'm all he has," she said simply. "He doesn't want me to be hurt again."

"Again?"

She nodded. "I told you that I had been married once."

"So he wants to keep you in a bottle?"

"It's not like that at all." Shannon sounded more sad than angry. "I don't expect you to understand. You've been surrounded by a big family all your life. My mother died when I was about Rachel's age and since then, it's been just the two of us."

Mitch considered this. "I can see why you've always been close."

"Not always," Shannon said in a strained voice. "Pop spent so much time with the business—buried himself in it, actually. I was lonely as a child and absolutely obnoxious as a teenager."

"You obnoxious?"

"Oh, yes." Shannon managed a thin smile. "Didn't you have teenage sisters?" She laughed as Mitch paled slightly, a look of empathy in his eyes. "Well, there you are. I was typical, I guess: rebellious and insecure. When Pop realized how far apart we'd drifted, he tried to make amends, but by then I wasn't particularly receptive. I turned my back on everything, left home and married the first man who asked me."

Mitch's chest suddenly felt too large for his skin. She looked so fragile, so forlorn. He imagined the solitary, frightened child-woman she must have been, and he experienced an irrational sense of anger at what she'd endured.

He brushed her hair with his fingertips. "I wish I'd known you then," he whispered. "I wouldn't have let anyone hurt you."

Surprised, she looked at him and their eyes locked. Shannon held his gaze, seeming to search his soul. He saw her confusion, her silent question. He cupped her face with his palm and felt her quiver beneath his touch.

Then she turned away and took a deep breath. Mitch allowed her the space she sought and returned his hand to the back of the park bench.

"So," Mitch said, his voice a bit ragged, "you're both trying to make up for lost time."

"It may seem like that. Lindsay certainly thinks so, but the fact is that we enjoy each other's company. Saturday is just kind of 'our day.'"

"You do his laundry and clean his house?"

Shannon's frown told Mitch that his tone was unappreciated.

"I'm sorry. It's none of my business." Not yet, he added silently, but it would be very much his business someday. Soon.

She relaxed. "I don't see it as a big deal. We usually do things together. But he never lets me cook for him."

"That bad?"

"Oh, yes."

Mitch cleared his throat. "So, what about Sundays?"

"What about them?"

"Well, do you have Sundays off? I mean, could I have your Sundays?" Mitch felt his face heat. He was stuttering like a pubescent nerd, every smooth verse perfected as a gender-war veteran seemed to have slipped out of his brain. Shannon stared at him as though he'd suddenly sprouted antlers. "The beach," he finally croaked. "Sunday. Would you like to go? With me? With us?"

Shannon was smiling now, in a tiny, twitching movement. Her green eyes sparkled. "I'd love to."

"You would?" She would. Wonderful. "Is eight o'clock too early? I'll pick you up."

Shannon shook her head. "That's out-of-the-way. I'll come over."

Mitch suspected that she simply wanted a bit more control of the situation, but he didn't argue. "Come hungry. We'll have breakfast first."

"Please don't bother on my account. I'll just grab a doughnut."

Mitch seemed horrified at the thought. "Why, that's nothing but junk food, empty calories. It's poison."

"I *like* doughnuts," she said defensively. "Unfortunately, so do my hips."

"And lovely hips they are," Mitch said. "I never did care for thin women."

"Oh, thank you so much."

"No! I meant that I prefer round women, like you."

Shannon's eyes were green slits.

Flinching, Mitch mumbled, "Uh, how about that breakfast?"

Rachel, who had been following the conversation with interest, could no longer contain herself. "I can help, Uncle

Mitch.'' She turned to Shannon. ''I can make pancakes all by myself.''

''You can?'' Shannon smoothed a brown lock off Rachel's forehead. ''Well, honey, you've got me beat. I don't do pancakes.''

''It's easy.'' Rachel brightened. ''I can teach you.''

''Umm . . . we'll see.''

There was a soft flicker, then warm light streamed from the lamps lining the walkway. Mitch was surprised to realize how dark it had gotten. He saw Shannon glance at her watch and knew it was time to leave.

But Sunday seemed so very far away.

THE ADVENTURES OF BIFF BARNETT,
PRIVATE INVESTIGATOR

Biff shimmies through the window of a warehouse where Rollo has been gagged and tied to a chair. Rollo's eyes are wide and frightened.

When Biff removes the gag, Rollo stutters, ''W-what do you want?''

''I want you to sing like a canary, pal,'' Biff tells him. ''And my favorite song is 'Pop Goes the Weasel.'''

Later at the precinct, Rollo hugs his children and looks gratefully at Biff. ''You saved my life. How can I ever repay you?''

''You got a couple of swell kids there,'' Biff says, looking embarrassed by the praise. ''Take good care of 'em.''

After Rollo and the children have gone, Maggie watches Biff turn away and wipe his eyes. She says, ''Well, big guy, I guess you're not such a hard-nose after all.''

''Keep it to yourself, Maggie,'' Biff mutters. ''I got a reputation to protect.''

The house was in chaos. Caesar the cat shot between Shannon's feet the moment Dusty opened the door and a cacophony of noise assaulted her. Dusty rolled his eyes, pointed toward the kitchen and retreated up the stairs at a dead run.

Trapped within the boring confines of her playpen, Stefie produced indignant shrieks that literally vibrated the living room. The toddler saw Shannon and threw her fat arms up in a plea for immediate release. "Up!" she begged. Shannon couldn't have resisted except that her attention was caught by the sound of pitiful sobbing from the kitchen.

Shannon followed the cries, ignoring Stefie's resentful wail of protest. She found Rachel wailing as though her little heart would break, refusing Mitch's attempts to soothe her.

Mitch looked miserable. "It's her pancakes," he said. The simple explanation left Shannon bewildered and set off a new round of hiccuping sobs.

"Oh, Rachel, what happened?"

Rachel flung herself into Shannon's arms. Shannon angled a questioning look at Mitch.

He raked at his hair. "We were out of pancake mix, so she decided to use flour." Mitch laid his hand on Rachel's quivering shoulder. It quivered harder. "Honey, it was an honest mistake. We'll make another batch."

"I'm confused," Shannon said. "Was something wrong with the flour?"

"Well, there was a bag of white powdery stuff on the pantry floor, but it wasn't exactly flour." Mitch stared morosely at the flat, white objects scattered across the counter. "It was plaster of Paris."

Shannon's eyes widened. Plaster pancakes? As the humor of the situation hit, Shannon bit her lip to keep from laughing. Her eyes locked with Mitch's and she saw his mouth twitch. His chest began to vibrate, then air whooshed from his lungs and he turned away, nearly choking in his attempt to maintain a sympathetic decorum.

Then Shannon lost it. She giggled once, swallowed, cleared her throat, then burst into laughter.

Rachel went rigid. She wiped at her eyes and glared first at Shannon, then at Mitch. Pulling away from Shannon, she stamped her foot in frustration. "It's not funny."

"Of course it is," Shannon said, picking up one of the saucerlike objects. "These are just like the pancakes *I* make."

Rachel blinked, then a small smile tweaked at the corner of her mouth. "You're just saying that."

Shannon raised her right hand. "Cross my heart."

Rachel giggled. "Oh, Shannon. You're funny."

Mitch was examining a plaster cake. "Actually, these are kind of neat." He opened the back door and called Snyder. The dog greeted him enthusiastically. "Catch, boy." With the easy wrist action of an experienced Frisbee flicker, Mitch sent the pancake sailing across the yard. Snyder, hot on its trail, leaped to grab the disk in his teeth, proudly retrieving his prize.

Rachel was delighted. The crisis was over.

A flurry of activity followed as they all gathered diapers, made sandwiches for lunch, grabbed sand pails and towels and other necessities for a day at the beach. They were just leaving when Shannon noticed the VCR's Record light was on. When she pointed it out to Mitch, he seemed strangely embarrassed, but was obviously aware that the machine was running, so Shannon promptly put it out of her mind.

Mitch, grumbling but half starved, relented on the doughnut issue, much to the children's delight. Shannon was still wiping powdered sugar from Stefie's face when they reached their destination.

The sand was warm and dry, the air balmy and mild. It was, Shannon decided, a perfect beach day. They'd spread their towels on a small sand rise with an unobstructed view of the surf.

Shannon pulled a small camera from her purse. "Smile!" Click. A perfect shot of Mitch tangled in towels. Shannon set the camera down long enough to help Mitch spread a blanket.

Stefie sat in the sand surrounded by a clever expandable fence-type structure that Mitch referred to as a portable playpen. Working on a sand castle, Rachel sat cautiously beyond the reach of the ocean's foaming tongues but Dusty was already in water up to his knees. Shannon's gaze was glued nervously on the seemingly fearless youngster.

"Don't go out any farther," she called to Dusty. "Be careful of the rip tides! Stay away from the surfers! Watch out for—"

"Sharks?" Mitch suggested. "Enemy submarines?"

Shannon flushed. "I've always been a big worrywart, I guess. It's just that the ocean's so big and he looks so small."

Mitch nodded wisely. "A natural motherly instinct."

Shannon's expression didn't reflect the impact she felt at his words. "I've decided that motherly instinct is not a natural phenomenon," she said carefully. "It's an acquired skill."

"What makes you say that?"

"Experience, I guess. When I was a little girl, I thought that parenting came naturally only to females and was a talent possessed equally by all members of my gender. You're the perfect example of the flaw in that logic."

"Me?"

"You handle the kids as though you've been doing it all your life."

Mitch laughed. "I *have* been doing it all my life."

"You see? It's an acquired skill."

"And you don't feel you've acquired it."

Shannon sifted the sand through her fingers. "When I married a man with a nine-year-old daughter, I accepted the challenge of instant motherhood with blind faith. It didn't work out."

"That's their loss, Shannon." Mitch slid his hand down Shannon's arm as he murmured, "And our good fortune."

His touch was as soft as a whisper, yet deeply stirring. Shannon was acutely aware of the man beside her. The thigh-length swimsuit he wore fit him well and flattered his lean frame. His spicy-musk scent mingled with the ocean's salt tang in an enveloping aura of sensuality. Something stirred deep within her, an aching need that unfurled and warmed and seeped into her very soul.

The sun's rays poured over her body, yet Shannon shivered. A loose cotton shirt covered her bathing suit and Mitch slowly peeled the fabric away. His eyes were mesmerizing, gripping hers with some inexplicable force. Shannon couldn't look away. She didn't want to.

When Mitch caressed her shoulders spreading the sweet fragrance of coconut, Shannon's skin quivered with delight. Body heat warmed the suntan oil as he massaged with smooth, circular movements. Her eyes fluttered shut. It was all too wonderful.

The shirt rippled to the sand. Shannon saw Mitch's gaze brush over her body and wondered if he was disappointed by the modest one-piece suit she'd worn. His eyes darkened. Shannon's heart beat faster.

A stream of oil danced over her legs. When Mitch stroked her thighs, she felt an electric jolt. Shannon gasped. Mitch pulled his hand away as though burned. He was breathing heavily and had a look of pure shock on his face.

"Uncle Mitch?" Rachel received only a garbled response, but it satisfied her. "See my sand house?" She pointed helpfully in the proper direction.

Two sets of unfocused eyes dutifully followed the small finger.

"Nice," croaked Mitch.

"Lovely," mumbled Shannon.

"Thank you." Rachel looked at the plastic bottle. "Can I have some oil?"

Shannon felt control of her limbs and brain returning. "Sure, honey. Sit here." Shannon patted the towel and Rachel sat beside her. "Hold your hair up. That's a good girl."

Mitch still seemed a bit unbalanced. "I, uh, I think I'll test the water."

He stood a bit shakily. With a thin smile, Mitch turned, ran toward the water and dived into the foamy surf.

Shannon returned her attention to oiling Rachel.

"You smell like my mommy," Rachel said. "Her hair smelled like apricots, too."

"It's probably my shampoo. Turn around and let's do the front."

Rachel's dark eyes were riveted on Shannon's face. "You're pretty," she remarked. "My mommy was pretty, too."

Shannon's heart wrenched. "Yes, she was, honey. She was beautiful."

"Did you know my mommy?"

"No, but I wish I had. I think I would have liked her very much."

"I can do the rest." Rachel took the bottle and nearly emptied it on her legs. The oil poured over her knees and puddled in the sand. "Mommy used to take me shopping and to the movies. We did girl things."

"Girl things?"

With an affirmative nod the child continued, "We made cookies and stuff. Once she let me help her paint a table. It was fun."

"Did you do things with your daddy, too?"

"Sure, but sometimes he and Dusty did boy things."

"What kind of boy things?"

Rachel shrugged. "You know, baseball and soccer. Daddy was Dusty's Little-League coach. Now, Uncle Mitch is."

Shannon was beginning to see the point of this conversation. "So Dusty still has someone to do boy things with, but Uncle Mitch can't do girl things with you?"

Rachel stared at her shiny knees and shrugged gently.

"Well, personally, I don't think there's any difference between girl things and boy things."

"You don't?"

"No. After all, boys can make cookies—look at how well Uncle Mitch bakes—and girls can play baseball." Shannon saw that Rachel was mulling that over. "The thing is, sometimes girls just need to talk to each other, right?"

Rachel smiled coyly. "Uh-huh."

"Would you like to do some girl things with me?" Shannon smiled as Rachel's little head bobbed enthusiastically. "Next Sunday, then, if it's okay with Uncle Mitch."

Two slim arms clamped around Shannon's neck. "Uncle Mitch won't mind, Shannon, honest. We'll have fun." With that promise, Rachel scooped up the plastic pail and scampered back to her sand house.

Then Mitch and Dusty, wet and laughing, raced toward Shannon. Mitch collapsed on the blanket as Dusty shook himself, raining Shannon with drops of seawater. She rewarded him with a well-aimed towel flick and Dusty squealed with delight.

Mitch stood and tried to pull Shannon up. "The water's great. Come on."

"I can't leave Stefie." Shannon liked the ocean, but only from a distance.

"Stefie's asleep and Dusty will stay right here, won't you, sport?"

Dusty was suddenly petulant. "You promised to help me look for seashells."

"We'll do that later," Mitch assured him.

Staring at Shannon with obvious displeasure, Dusty said, "I want to do it now. You promised."

Shannon intervened. "It's all right, Mitch. I really don't mind staying here." The boy's childish frustration alarmed her. For a moment, Dusty had reminded Shannon of her stepdaughter. She held her breath.

Still watching Dusty, Mitch's eyes narrowed. "It's later or not at all, and I don't like your tone, young man."

Fidgeting in the sand, Dusty mumbled, "Sorry."

The petulant sulk was gone and Shannon sighed with relief.

"That's better, sport." Mitch tousled Dusty's hair. "Now, how about watching your sister for a while?"

"Sure." Dusty pulled an apple out of the lunch sack. "I'm tired anyway."

Shannon was stuck. "Maybe I'll just wade a bit—Mitch! Wait!"

Mitch had scooped Shannon into his arms and was running full speed toward the water. She had no choice but to cling to him as he jogged into the rushing waves. When the water reached his waist, he stopped, lifting her higher against his chest.

Shannon buried her face against his neck. His skin was slightly stubbled and she found the friction against her cheek pleasing.

The shallows were crowded with bathers, but Mitch carried her beyond the breakers, out to where the water rolled with gentle swells. As each wave rose beneath them, they caught a glimpse of the white beach before the water crested to block their view. Then they were isolated and alone.

Mitch loosened his grip, allowing her lower body to slide against his until her feet sank into the sandy bottom. Mitch held her waist and they floated over the slick swells, laughing. Then the laughter died and they gazed at each other as though something magical was happening. Slowly Mitch lowered his head, hesitated, then brought his lips to hers in a deep, sweet kiss.

Her pulse leaped and she was stunned by the impact of her own response. The kiss had been soft and gentle, but its effect had been potent, almost frightening.

Tomorrow, Shannon would analyze the implications of this moment. Now, she wanted only to cherish it.

They gazed at each other, their eyes locked in silent communion as though they were the only people in existence. Then a sound broke their trance.

Blinking like two somnambulists, they suddenly realized they were no longer alone. A grinning teenager floated on a surfboard a few feet away. The boy gave Mitch a look of grudging respect. "Nice moves, man," the boy said. "Real nice." Then he offered Mitch a thumbs-up sign, turned his board and paddled away.

Shannon knew her cheeks looked like ripe tomatoes. "I think we'd be safer back on dry land."

"We're not going to feel any differently."

"Maybe not, but at least we won't drown."

"Not a bad way to go."

"You're impossible." With a burst of self-discipline, Shannon managed to turn away. She felt Mitch's arm circle her waist as they sloshed toward the shore. When the water slapped softly against their ankles, he stopped her with a touch.

"Shannon—" He stared helplessly. What was wrong with him, anyway? His tongue was tangled in his teeth, his mouth was as dry as the Mojave Desert and his legs felt like wet strings.

Tilting her head, Shannon looked up expectantly. "What is it, Mitch?"

"Ah, I don't exactly know." He coughed nervously, then cleared his throat. "I feel kind of strange."

Her eyes darkened curiously, turning from the color of new leaves to a deep emerald. Mitch sucked in air, held his breath, then let it slide out through his teeth.

Raising a hand, he grazed her cheek with his knuckles. "You're so different, so very special...." Mitch's voice faded, to be replaced by a tight laugh. "The truth is, lady, you scare me to death."

Stunned, Shannon searched his expression and saw the honesty of his words. She felt him tremble. He had opened himself to her, shared his feelings, his fear. He was vulnerable and she knew that a thoughtless look, a careless word, could wound him to the core.

And with his surrender came triumph. He had captured her heart.

Chapter Five

Certified Mail. Return Receipt Requested.

The Gilberts had left nothing to chance. Mitch stared at the letter, as though reading it for the fifth time would change its meaning. It wouldn't. The document was from the Gilberts' attorney and officially declared their intent to challenge Mitch's status as the children's guardian.

Ross had told Mitch that the letter might merely be a legal maneuver, some tactic to manipulate Mitch into transferring custody and avoid the adverse publicity of a trial. In other words, the Gilberts were betting that Mitch would value his career and his personal reputation over the children's happiness.

"You're in for a bit of a surprise, Ruth," Mitch muttered. "And one hell of a fight."

He wadded the paper and flung it across the room. How dare they use three innocent kids this way? Mitch stood, pushing his drafting stool so hard it nearly fell over. He paced the office, fuming. It wasn't that he was unsympathetic to the Gilberts' grief over the loss of their only child. Mitch could even understand their desperation to fill that void with their daughter's children. What he couldn't understand was how they could ignore the harm this battle would do to those very children. The kids had lost their parents, for God's sake, and the Gilberts were trying to take them away from their familiar home and what remained of the family they'd grown up with.

No way. No damned way.

Mitch fingered his shiny black-and-brass oboe. As he raised it to his lips, he heard a raspy whirring followed by the constant thud of a hammer. He hesitated, listening. Mitch was aware that Shannon and Rachel were involved in some kind of project, but exactly what on earth were they up to?

Nestling the oboe in its case, Mitch followed the invading sounds. When he reached the kitchen, he glanced out the window and froze. He must be seeing things.

Shannon looked up, grinned and motioned him to come out.

"What do you think?" she asked when he stood, open-mouthed, in front of her. Plywood cutouts were strewn on the lawn, a large blueprint was spread over the patio table and Rachel sat on the ground happily sanding a wooden dowel.

Mitch found his voice. "What is this, this...?" His hands flapped helplessly as his voice trailed off.

Rachel wiggled her sandpaper. "We're doing girl things."

Shannon laughed. "Her term, not mine," she told Mitch. "Actually, we're building a doghouse for Snyder." She pointed to the blueprints. "Rachel and I wanted something that would blend with the architecture of the main house, so it will be a miniature Victorian."

Mitch studied the plans. It was a doghouse, all right, complete with covered porch and a large attic turret. "You've got to be joking," he said. "This isn't an afternoon project. It's a major construction job. I've seen condominiums that weren't this complex."

"It won't take as long as you think," Shannon replied. "I made the primary cutouts last week, so all we have to do is sand off the rough edges and put it together."

Mitch detected a bluish cast below Shannon's eyes. "When did you have time to do all that?"

"A little midnight oil and voilà. I like to keep busy."

"You look tired," Mitch remarked in a scolding tone. "You're stretching yourself too thin."

Shannon squinted up. "*You* should talk. You look like the subject of a sleep-deprivation experiment."

Now wanting to be left out, Rachel said, "Shannon says we can paint it next week and then it will be all done. Do you think Snyder will like it?"

"Uh, I'm sure he will, honey." Mitch glanced at the plans, then mumbled, "This darn thing is bigger than my first apartment."

Shannon smiled sweetly. "Snyder is a large dog."

At the sound of his name, Snyder swished his shaggy tail and broke his muzzle into a tongue-lolling, dog-type grin. He barked in apparent agreement.

Mitch was in shock. Shannon hadn't been exaggerating when she'd said carpentry was one of her hobbies. Mitch himself barely knew the difference between a claw hammer and a sledge hammer, but the tools Shannon had brought were impressive, probably of professional quality.

Dusty came out, watched briefly, then said, "Can I help?"

"No, this is girl stuff," Rachel told him.

Shannon tried to soothe them both. "Now, Rae, there's plenty of work for everyone."

"Forget it. It's dumb anyway." With that pronouncement, Dusty slammed into the house.

Mitch started to follow, but a swatch of plush, powder-blue carpeting caught his eye. "Tell me that's not what I think it is."

Shannon followed his gaze and smiled. "Don't you like the color?"

"You're going to carpet a dog house," he said flatly. "This is incredible. Will it have indoor plumbing?"

Rachel stopped sanding. "That's silly, Uncle Mitch." Round eyes regarded him with impatience. "Snyder doesn't know how to use faucets."

Mitch saw Shannon's mouth quiver, then she turned away and busied herself with a measuring tape.

"Why couldn't you just bake cookies?" Mitch mumbled, more to himself than to Shannon. She heard him, though, and shot him a look of pure annoyance.

"It would serve you right if I did," she said. "What seems to be your problem?"

"No problem," Mitch replied hastily. "It's just all a bit unexpected, that's all."

Shannon cocked her head, watching him thoughtfully. "Old Biff Barnett wouldn't approve of this, would he?"

Mitch frowned. "What does that mean?"

"Out of curiosity, I hit the library and researched your cartoon strip for the past year."

Mitch's internal caution lights began to glow in warning. Shannon's voice was level enough, but he detected an undercurrent of disapproval.

"Well, what do you think?" he asked warily.

She shrugged. "Biff seems to be mellowing a bit but he still refers to women in rather trite terms. Quite unflattering, actually."

With a long-suffering sigh, Mitch said, "Look, I've tried to explain this to the children's grandparents. I am *not* Biff Barnett. He's a cartoon character, for heaven's sake, and he relates to women in the heavy-handed, stereotypical manner his fans expect." He walked over to Shannon and traced the curve of her jaw with his fingertip. "If you've been following Biff, you know the plots all revolve around his crime-solving abilities. If he once ordered his secretary to get coffee for him or drooled over a good-looking woman, well, that macho behavior is part of his character. Besides, as you've already noticed, Biff *is* changing."

Shannon was listening carefully, almost too carefully. Her scrutiny made him strangely uncomfortable.

Finally her expression softened. "I guess I can understand your dilemma—"

Mitch cupped her chin in his palm. "But?"

"But . . . I don't know. Forget it." She lowered her eyelids. "Before I met you, I hadn't looked at a comics page in years. And I really don't know a thing about the cartoon business. I shouldn't have said anything."

"You can say anything you feel, anytime you want." He saw her lips part, felt a small shudder run through her. "I care about you, Shannon, and I respect your feelings."

The air turned heavy, charged with current. A gnawing ache twisted deep within her, passion tempered by tenderness, desire honed by anticipation.

"Shannon? I'm done," Rachel said impatiently.

Shannon blinked. "Umm? Oh, all right. I'll be right there." With a final shy glance at Mitch, she turned away.

Watching Shannon, Mitch decided that she looked better in sawdust than most women did in furs. So what if she was a bit unconventional and definitely not your everyday pie-baking domestic type? He could handle that. And Mitch had to admit that his niece hadn't seemed so animated or so happy in months. Shannon was good for Rachel.

She was good for Mitch, too.

A rustling sound captured Mitch's attention. An old mulberry tree shaded the rear of the large backyard and some of its limbs reached over the fence into the alley beyond. Those same limbs seemed to be moving.

Snyder, too, was interested in the activity beyond the wall. The animal sat under the tree and studied a vibrating branch.

Mitch heard the sound of hushed laughter, then two young faces appeared and peeked over the fence. Mitch recognized one of the girls as a neighbor's daughter. What was her name—Kelly?

"Look," shrieked the unfamiliar girl. "It's him. It's really *him*."

"I told you," Kelly said smugly, then waved cheerfully. "Yoo-hoo, Mr. Wheeler! Could my friend, Marci, please have your autograph?"

Snyder barked a happy welcome and wagged his tail with enthusiasm. Thus encouraged, the girls pulled themselves up and sat, clapping and squealing, on the stone wall.

Groaning, Mitch slid a glance at Shannon. She was staring openmouthed at the teenagers looking stunned, but Mitch noted that she didn't look pleased. With a helpless gesture, he marched across the yard. As he approached the wall, Marci giggled ecstatically and thrust out her autograph book.

Mitch took the book and shot the girls what he hoped was a sternly reproachful look. "If I sign this, will you promise never to invade anyone else's privacy like this?"

Two heads bobbed in unison. "We promise," they chimed, then broke into a renewed fit of giggles.

Scrawling his name across the page, Mitch handed the book back. "Now, young ladies, if you'll kindly remove yourselves from my fence—"

"Oh, wow! Like, this is so totally rad."

"Thanks, Mr. Wheeler. You're really super."

There was a flutter of ponytails and suntanned legs, and the teenagers disappeared. Mitch heard fading footsteps as they ran down the alley.

That was ill-timed, Mitch thought, and he wondered how Shannon felt about the embarrassing scene. He glanced across the yard and tried to look pleasant.

Shannon didn't return his smile. Mitch had been patient, she knew, and she also realized that he'd been less than thrilled by the intrusion. Still, it had been a shock to face such tangible, undeniable evidence of Mitch's celebrity status.

She was aware that the incident hadn't been Mitch's fault. He had no control over the behavior of overly exuberant fans—just as Shannon couldn't have controlled the media invasion that had followed her own divorce. She remembered the flashbulbs exploding through windows, reporters hiding in her father's yard, waiting like vultures for a death scent.

In the years that followed, Shannon had immersed herself in blissful obscurity. Now she saw that anonymity slipping away. As long as she was with Mitch, she would be subject to the same scrutiny as a bug in a bottle. The realization was horrifying.

Quickly thumbing through the newspaper, Shannon found the section she sought and spread it on the living room floor. Dusty sprawled beside her. As promised last Sunday, Shannon had helped Rachel finish the doghouse. Now, Rachel was upstairs trying to scour dried paint off her hands.

Dusty had seemed quiet today, Shannon noted, almost as if he were resentful of the time she and Rachel were spending together. To engage Dusty in conversation, Shannon had asked him about school. Soon she'd found herself relating her own classroom experiences. She'd mentioned that her major was economics, one thing had led to another and now she was explaining the fundamental theories of the Dow Jones Index. She was pleased by his interest. Of course, the lesson had to be simplified a bit, put in terms a seven-year-old mind could identify with, but Dusty seemed enthusiastic.

Shannon was using a bowl of mixed fruit to define the composition of a mutual fund, when she saw Mitch watching them with an expression of disbelief.

"Hi, Uncle Mitch. I'm learning 'nomics."

"Oh. Well, that's fine, sport, but you'd better get into uniform. The game starts in an hour."

"Okay." Dusty scrambled to his feet. "See you later, Shannon." He disappeared up the stairs.

Mitch arched one eyebrow. "'Nomics?"

"Economics. Dusty and I were comparing notes on school."

"Ah." Mitch knelt to help Shannon refold the newspaper. "Why did you decide to go back to college?"

"It wasn't really a question of going back so much as starting in the first place." She neatly squared the stack of papers and laid them on the coffee table. "After high school, I didn't really know what I wanted to do, but I was sick of studying so I went to work."

"Doing what?"

"I was a waitress for a while, then I sold perfume in a department store." She smiled. "Not the stuff of which careers are made."

"You didn't work for your father?"

"No. We weren't getting along." The memory of those years saddened Shannon. "It wasn't until after my divorce that Pop and I really began to communicate. I learned the plumbing business from the ground up, then realized that I wanted to see it expanded, modernized. That required knowledge, so I went to the university and passed the entrance exams."

"How long until you get your degree?"

"Another year. It takes longer at night. I can't handle as many semester units as a full-time student can. There aren't enough hours in the day."

Mitch was silent, but Shannon could almost hear the gears in his brain turning. "It all seems so much. You work a full day, then attend classes three nights a week and every time I manage to get you on the phone, you're too busy to talk."

Where was this leading? Shannon wondered.

"I mean, a bachelor's degree is hardly a requirement for repairing pipes," Mitch said, his voice like silk. "There are more pleasant ways to spend your evenings."

"Oh?"

Mitch lifted her hand and brushed his lips across her palm. "I'm just being selfish, I suppose, but I'd like to spend more time with you." His teeth nipped on the fleshy pad below her thumb and she shivered at the exquisite sensation. "Would you like that?"

She managed to nod. The man was driving her wild.

"Why don't you come with us this afternoon?" Mitch said.

"To Dusty's soccer game?"

"Sure. Dusty would be thrilled to have a rooting section."

Shannon doubted that. She'd already noticed that Dusty was exhibiting symptoms of possessiveness toward his Uncle Mitch and suspected that the boy would be upset to share him. "What about the girls?"

"I usually take them to my sister's house on soccer days." He smiled lazily. "I'm sure she'd watch Dusty after the game. We could have an evening together."

Shannon pushed thoughts of Dusty's jealousy from her mind. An evening with Mitch was tempting, no doubt about it. Too tempting. Shannon knew what could happen if she and Mitch were alone for a few hours and she wasn't at all certain she was ready for such a major change in their relationship. "I have a better idea," she said.

Mitch perked up, interested.

"You take Dusty to the game, Stefie will stay with your sister and I'll take Rachel out to dinner and a movie."

Mitch's face fell. "You're joking."

"Not at all." Shannon was serious now. "She's so lonely, Mitch, and she misses her mother. I'd like to make her feel special for a few hours."

Mitch regarded Shannon thoughtfully. "You're right. She's such a quiet child, such a good little girl, I just never realized—" He looked away, his eyes filled with pain. "Am I wrong to want them with me, Shannon? Should I let them go?"

His expression tore at her heart. "No, Mitch, you're not wrong." Instinctively, her arms encircled him, resting his head against her breast. "Those children adore you."

And so do I, she added silently. So do I.

"Rachel, honey, wake up. We're home."

Shannon opened the passenger door and scooped up the yawning child. As tiny arms wound around Shannon's neck, she felt a peculiar surge, a strange sense of protectiveness mingled with something else that she couldn't quite identify. A motherly instinct? No, of course not. Shannon had already determined that there was probably no such thing and even if there was, she certainly didn't possess it. The experience with her stepdaughter had reinforced that conviction.

"I can walk," Rachel mumbled, but even as she spoke, her little head sank to Shannon's shoulder.

Shannon pushed the car door shut with her foot and carried Rachel to the porch. From inside the house, Shannon heard the sound of zooming airplanes, gunfire and excited voices. It was loud enough to wake neighbors three blocks away and she decided that Mitch must be watching some old movie on television. She bent awkwardly to twist the doorknob with the hand that held Rachel's knees.

Quietly easing through the front door, Shannon carried Rachel toward the den, then stopped, stunned at what she saw. The television was on, all right, but it wasn't tuned to a movie. Colorful cartoons splashed across the screen, spaceships with batlike wings, a robot gorilla chewing scrap metal and a family of bionic beings fighting the evil of the world with iron-knuckled minirockets. Beside the screen, a VCR whirred happily and Mitch Wheeler, grown adult male, was seated on the floor, pigging out on popcorn and cheering like an enraptured six-year-old.

Shannon could only stare.

It could be worse, she finally decided. He could have been playing his oboe.

Rachel's head wobbled up. She squinted toward the television screen and yawned. "We saw *Bambi*, Uncle Mitch, and we had pizza and hot fudge sundaes and—" She interrupted herself with another yawn.

Mitch leaped to his feet, hitting the television's "off" button while trying to kick the popcorn bowl under the coffee table. He managed a nervous grin, raked at his hair and cleared his throat. "I didn't expect you so soon."

Shannon's expression was deliberately blank, but her eyes sparkled with amusement. "It's after ten."

"Oh."

Silence. Mitch shifted uncomfortably as Shannon's gaze swept from the VCR, piled with carefully labeled tapes, to stray popcorn kernels adorning the carpet. Apparently there was at least one exception to Mitch's professed aversion to junk food.

A thought struck Shannon as she saw Mitch's obvious embarrassment at being caught. "So that's why the VCR is always recording on Sunday mornings."

"Research," Mitch mumbled, then gathered the sleepy child in his arms. "I'll just get her into bed."

Shannon watched Mitch carry Rachel up the stairs, then dropped her purse on the sofa and wandered over to the stack of tapes. Mitch had quite a collection—*The Masked Avenger*, *Silverhawks*, *Defenders of the Earth*. Amazing! Shannon wondered what the tabloids would say about the real Mitch Wheeler, the man who tucks a sleepy little girl into bed, coaches a peewee soccer team and has a secret fetish for his favorite cartoon superheroes. She decided that the "dig-for-dirt" magazines probably wouldn't be interested in this Mitch Wheeler. It was all too mundane to be splashed across the headlines. They preferred Mitch as glitzy ladies' man, and glamorous talk-show guest.

Which was real? Shannon realized that she'd been only too willing to believe those headlines, even though she knew from painful personal experience just how distorted such journalism could be. It was a sad commentary on her own prejudice, a streak of blind judgment she hadn't even realized was a part of her. If Mitch himself hadn't been so insistent, Shannon might never have seen beyond the superficial hype.

She grew cold at the thought. Suddenly Shannon could no longer visualize a life without Mitch and the children. It was a complication she hadn't anticipated.

"She was asleep before her head hit the pillow."

Startled by Mitch's voice, Shannon whirled to see him standing behind her—close. Her breath caught against her tonsils at the sight of him, the scent of him. The VCR tape slipped from her fingers and bounced softly across the carpet. Neither seemed to notice.

"I missed you," Mitch murmured, stroking her cheek with his finger.

"I, that is, *we* missed you, too." Shannon felt a twinge of panic. She *had* missed Mitch. In fact, she missed him every moment of the days when they couldn't be together. This man was dominating her thoughts. The power he had over her mind, over her life, was suddenly frightening.

His lips brushed her mouth, gently, sweetly, then clung as he kissed her deeply. She responded without conscious thought, pulling him closer as he molded her body against his. He tasted warm and buttery, with a light, salty tang. Popcorn had never felt so erotic.

When the kiss ended, Shannon was trembling. She felt the telltale quiver of Mitch's hand cupping her face and knew that he, too, was affected.

"Shannon, honey." The words came out in a hoarse croak and Mitch took a deep breath. "Something is happening between us that can't be ignored. We need to talk about it."

Shannon's knees felt like water. She didn't want to talk about it. She wanted—no, she needed to *think*, but her brain didn't function properly when Mitch was so close.

Turning away, she steadied herself against the sofa. "It's late. I have to go."

"Tomorrow, then."

She grabbed her purse. "Tomorrow is Monday. I have classes."

"Wait." Mitch snagged her arm and she bounced against his chest. He held her there. "We need some time together. Alone."

Mitch's voice was low and silky, stroking her like a soft feather. She shivered and moistened her suddenly dry lips.

"This feeling isn't going to disappear," Mitch said. "You can't fight it by running away."

"I'm not running away."

"You're trying to, but I won't let you."

She stiffened at the truth of his statement. "This is all new to me. I honestly don't know how to react, what to do."

Mitch chuckled. "It's new to me, too. In fact, I've never felt this way before and frankly, it's even scarier than being an instant father. But I'm willing to face my feelings, Shannon." He gently lifted her chin with his thumb and looked straight into her eyes. "Are you?"

Was she? Was she willing to face the fact that she was falling in love with this man? Was she willing to gamble her heart again?

Mitch looked up from his drafting table and saw Ross Wheeler standing in the doorway of his studio. Mitch noted that as usual, his brother was in full lawyer-type garb, from perfectly tailored gray suit to appropriately grim expression.

Replacing the ink pen in its holder, Mitch swiveled the highboy stool and watched as Ross set his briefcase on the desk. Mitch wasn't particularly surprised to see Ross. His brother had a key to the house and frequently let himself in, especially during Mitch's working hours.

Ross tilted his head, as though listening. "It's strangely quiet today."

"Dusty and Rachel are in school. Stefie's in the middle of one of her rare naps, so I was able to get an extra hour of work in."

"Oh." Ross was obviously disappointed. Mitch knew that for all his brother's outward stiffness, Ross was enormously fond of the children and looked forward to seeing them. As the oldest of the Wheeler's six siblings, Ross had been just twenty when their parents had died and he'd taken on the role of family patriarch. Over the years, Ross had developed a deeply ingrained feeling of responsibility toward the entire Wheeler clan.

As a youngster, Mitch had idolized his older brother. If Ross's protective nature had on occasion bordered on annoyance and meddlesomeness, Mitch had been tolerant.

After all, Ross had suffered more than his share of tragedy.

When Ross's ex-wife had spirited his own children away, Ross had been completely shattered. After four years, Ross hadn't given up hope of someday locating his daughters but had compensated for their absence by showering affection on his many nieces and nephews.

With the blink of an eye, Ross, The Uncle, was replaced by Ross, The Lawyer. "The syndication contracts came through today." Ross briskly snapped open his case and rifled through a sheaf of papers. "I've taken the liberty of amending some of the clauses and I'd suggest—"

"Good morning, Ross," Mitch said cheerfully. "And how are you today?"

Ross frowned. "I'm busy, thank you, and since it's obvious that you're busy, as well, I'd just as soon skip the amenities. Now, about these contracts—"

"We may be family, but that's no reason to ignore the fact that this is a beautiful day and life is wonderful." Mitch pulled at the fingerless glove that protected his drawing hand from ink. "As soon as I finish this strip, I'll be nearly caught up."

"And that is the reason for your disgustingly cheerful mood?"

Mitch grinned. "Not entirely, but it helps."

Grumbling, Ross strode across the room and examined Mitch's completed work. A corkboard covered the wall behind the drafting table and a half a dozen cartoon strips, fully inked and signed, were tacked up. The drawings were approximately twice the size of the reduced strips that would appear in the comics pages.

"What's going on here?" Ross asked. "I thought your esteemed Mr. Barnett had just rescued some poor unfortunate clod from evil mobsters."

"That's the plot that's running in the newspapers right now," Mitch explained patiently. "This is the next story line. What do you think?"

Ross studied the board. "I'd be the first to admit that action-adventure heroes are not my forte, but—"

"But what?"

"Hasn't old Biff been getting a bit, ah, soft?"

"Soft? Because he expresses his feelings? I think it makes him more human." Mitch winced at the term and added, "Sort of human, anyway."

Ross pursed his lips. "Well, you're the artist, of course, and if you believe his fans will accept a Biff romance, so be it."

Folding his arms in a gesture of annoyance, Mitch asked, "Would you prefer Biff to hire another secretary?"

That got Ross's attention. "Lord, no! You don't need the feminists picketing the publishers again."

Mitch regarded Ross sullenly. "I don't even know what they were protesting in the first place."

"Did you really think that forcing secretarial applicants to make coffee instead of taking a typing test would endear you to the working women of the world?"

With a sound of disgust, Mitch tossed his arms in the air. "Feminists, conservationists, liberals, moderates—I can't please everyone. It's a cartoon strip, not a commentary."

"Politics isn't exclusive to politicians, Mitchell. You have access to people's homes, to their minds. That carries an immense responsibility."

"Are you implying that I'm shirking my responsibilities?"

"No, but I'm suggesting that Biff's adventures have usually paralleled major events in your own life. Caricatured and parodied, of course, but the similarities are undeniable."

Mitch took a sharp breath. "Art may imitate life, but I am *not* Biff Barnett."

As Ross stared at the storyboard, his expression tightened. "I hope not," he finally murmured. "I sincerely hope not." Then with a blink, Ross turned to Mitch. "Now, about those contracts."

Mitch snatched the papers out of Ross's hand, read them, then signed with a flourish. "How about some coffee? I've made a decision and you get to be the first to know."

Ross stiffened. "I don't like the sound of that."

"You don't like anything that isn't typed in triplicate and couched in blue legal paper." An electric coffeepot sat on the desk and Mitch poured two cupfuls.

Ross took a proffered cup and sipped the hot brew. "All right, I'm braced. What's your big news?"

Mitch sat on the edge of the desk, feeling immensely pleased with himself. The decision had been so simple, really. Most of his life, Mitch had never even considered the option. It was always a "someday" kind of thing, a "when the time is right." Mitch's life had changed dramatically in the past few months. He had responsibilities now, he had a family. He had Shannon. Yes, the time was definitely right.

Mitch regarded his brother thoughtfully. "I'm thinking of getting married."

Ross choked on his coffee. "Are you insane?" Pulling a crisp white handkerchief from his pinstriped pocket, Ross alternately wiped at his coffee-stained suit and sputtered at Mitch. Suddenly, Ross's hand froze in midwipe. "It's not the plumber."

Mitch straightened. "If you mean Shannon, yes, it most certainly is."

"Oh, God." Ross paled, staring back at the storyboard, then rubbed his eyes and muttered, "I knew it."

"What?"

"Look, I can understand how difficult it's been for you, trying to care for three children and maintain your career, but surely there's another alternative. Marriage is a rather drastic step, wouldn't you agree? Can't you just hire a nanny or something?"

"That's ridiculous."

"Is it? There have been a passel of beauties in your life and you've never felt a burning need to marry any of them."

Ross fixed his brother with a penetrating stare. "This isn't going to solve your problem with the children's grandparents."

"Maybe not, but it won't hurt."

"You've only known this woman for a few weeks. At least wait until this business with the Gilberts is settled before you make a decision."

"Why? You said yourself that a stable relationship could be beneficial to my position. Well, marriage is as stable as it gets."

"Do you think it's fair to marry this woman merely to improve your chances in court?"

"That's absurd." Mitch tried to be reasonable. "Do you remember how Mom and Dad were together?"

"Of course, but they had a very unusual, very special relationship."

"Well, that's what I want." Mitch's voice softened as he visualized Shannon comforting Dusty, building a doghouse with Rachel and washing Stefie's sticky hands. "That's what Shannon wants, too."

Ross was obviously agitated. "I haven't heard the word *love* mentioned, and although I'd be the first to acknowledge that such maudlin emotion alone is a poor reason for a lifetime commitment, one usually takes it into consideration."

"I don't know why I expected you to understand," Mitch said grimly. "You've never even met Shannon so you haven't a clue as to what kind of woman she is. She's perfect for the children and perfect for me. I'm going to ask her to marry me and that is simply that."

Ross picked up on the last sentence with interest. "Shall I interpret that to mean you haven't actually, er, popped the question?"

"Well, not exactly."

"Then perhaps my concern is a bit premature." Ross rubbed his hands together like a fly on a sugar cube. "When, exactly, were you planning to do so?"

"Tonight. I've got tickets to *Les Misérables* at the Shubert Theater and reservations for a late supper afterward." Mitch tossed his brother a pleading look and added, "You're not going to back out on your promise to baby-sit, are you?"

"I'll be here as planned." Suddenly Ross seemed a bit too relaxed. "Perhaps the lady will use more common sense in this situation than you have thus far."

"And what is that supposed to mean?"

"Has it occurred to you that she might refuse?"

Mitch was shocked. "No, it hasn't."

"Quite the confident devil, aren't you?" Ross's expression was infuriatingly smug. Straightening his tie, he retrieved the contract and filed the document in his neatly organized briefcase. "As your brother, I hope that you and the lady have a delightful evening. As your counsel of record, however, I strongly recommend that you postpone any long-term commitments until your other legal problems are under control." Ross gave Mitch a direct stare. "If it will give my advice more credence, I'll bill you for it."

With that, Ross turned and strode out of the house.

Mitch sat at the drafting table and picked up the ink pen. He stared sightlessly at his work. Could Ross have been right? What if Shannon wouldn't marry him?

No, she wouldn't refuse. He remembered how her body quivered when he touched her, how her eyes darkened with desire. Besides, Shannon adored the children and was natural with them, knowing instinctively what made each of them unique and how to relate to that individuality. And hadn't she told him that day at the beach how much she'd wanted a large family? They had the same traditional values, the same goals in life.

It's settled, then, Mitch decided. Why would she refuse to marry him when it was all so logical? She wouldn't, of course. Ross was just being his normal, gloom-and-doom self.

Mitch stared at the vibrating ink pen and realized that his hands were shaking.

Chapter Six

Lindsay cocked her head at the two bedraggled plumbers. "Well, it's about time. Frank has been clock-watching since three."

Shannon dropped her tool case on the lobby floor and pushed a damp strand of hair from her forehead. "Rerouting an entire plumbing system takes time." She turned to the tall man beside her. "Good job, Mike. Punch on out and I'll finish the paperwork."

Mike seemed relieved. He gave Shannon a grateful smile, waved at Lindsay and headed for the locker room.

"Big job, eh?" Lindsay rested her chin in her hands. "The work order just said, 'Undefined leakage.'"

"That leakage turned out to be a pipe break in the concrete slab," Shannon said. "We had to cap the main system into the house, dig a ditch halfway to China and lay an alternate pipe around the foundation." Shannon collapsed into a chair beside Lindsay's desk. "I realize I have to learn the business from the ground up, but this is ridiculous."

Lindsay chuckled. "No one said it would be easy. Someday, when you've traded that cute little blue jumpsuit for pinstripes, you'll laugh about this."

"Umm." Shannon stretched, moaning as her stiff muscles rebelled. "I can't wait to sink into a hot bath and soak until I turn pruney."

"Not too pruney," Lindsay cautioned. "You've got a date with Mitch, don't you?"

"Yes. And he's being very secretive about it. He just told me to get dressed for a night on the town and he'd pick me up at seven."

"Sounds encouraging." A round bowl filled with jelly beans sat on the corner of the desk and Lindsay poked through it. "Someone got all the green ones. Probably Frank, the fink." Lindsay shrugged and popped a pink bean into her mouth. She ate the candy, then said, "You like him a lot, don't you?"

Shannon blinked. "Of course. He's my father."

"Not Frank. Mitch."

"Oh." Shannon's expression softened. "Yes, Linnie, I like him a lot." That was an understatement, Shannon realized. Mitch Wheeler dominated her thoughts and her dreams. They'd met less than a month ago, but to Shannon it had seemed a lifetime. Every aspect of her world had changed; her priorities had shifted. The university studies that had been such a joy to her were now a burden. She resented the time they required—time that she could have shared with Mitch. And the children.

The children. They'd come to mean so much to her. After the divorce, Shannon had felt as though she would never be able to relate to children again. She had lost confidence in her own abilities with them and she'd mistrusted their motives. But with Dusty and Rachel and even little Stefie . . . well, Shannon was finally able to believe that her failure with Trudy might have been an isolated incident.

Lindsay made a hissing sound that startled Shannon back to the present.

"Oh, Lord, be still, my heart." Lindsay's chin dropped as she stared out the glass lobby door into the parking lot. "Now *there* is a fine specimen."

Shannon followed Lindsay's admiring gaze and saw a distinguished looking man clutching a briefcase as he strode purposefully toward the building. Impeccably dressed in a no-nonsense gray suit, he would have been strikingly handsome had it not been for his grim expression.

Lindsay was fanning herself with her hand. "What a hunk! He can put his briefcase under my desk anytime. Good grief, he's coming in here!" She pushed a stray lock behind her ear, automatically smoothed her skirt and flashed her sweetest "Well, hello there" smile as the man opened the lobby door. "Good afternoon, sir. May I help you?"

Amazed by Lindsay's abrupt transformation, Shannon could only stare. It was unlike Lindsay to be awestruck by the mere sight of a man—any man.

This particular man stood with the straight spine of a soldier and the cool eyes of a general. His gaze scanned the room with something akin to disdain, then rested on Lindsay's now composed face. "Ross Wheeler to see Ms. Doherty," he said formally.

Shannon felt her jaw sag. Ross Wheeler? Quickly she looked at Lindsay, who, bless her, had managed to keep her expression professionally impassive.

"Do you have an appointment, Mr. Wheeler?" Lindsay inquired politely.

Only a thin crease of his brow indicated Ross Wheeler's impatience. "No. But I'd hoped she would be able to spare me a few moments."

"I see." Lindsay subtly glanced toward Shannon, offering her a way out. A mere shake of Shannon's head and Lindsay would send the rigid Mr. Wheeler on his way.

Shannon was tempted. She was grimy and disheveled, still in her grungy uniform. This was definitely not the manner in which she wanted to greet Mitch's older brother. The temptation was short-lived, however. She was sitting two

SILHOUETTE GIVES YOU SIX REASONS TO CELEBRATE!

MAIL THE BALLOON TODAY!

INCLUDING:

1.
4 FREE BOOKS

2.
A LOVELY 20k GOLD ELECTROPLATED CHAIN

3.
A SURPRISE BONUS

AND MORE!

TAKE A LOOK...

Yes, become a Silhouette subscriber and the celebration goes on forever.

To begin with we'll send you:

4 new Silhouette Romance™ novels — FREE

a lovely 20k gold electroplated chain—FREE

an exciting mystery bonus—FREE

And that's not all! Special extras— Three more reasons to celebrate.

4. **CONVENIENT Home Delivery!** That's right! We'll send you 4 FREE books, and you'll be under no obligation to purchase any in the future. You may keep the books and return the accompanying statement marked cancel.

If we don't hear from you, about a month later we'll send you six additional novels to read and enjoy. If you decide to keep them, you'll pay the already low price of just $2.25* each — plus only 69 cents delivery for the entire shipment. There are **no** hidden extras! **You may cancel at any time!** But as long as you wish to continue, every month we'll send you six more books, which you can purchase or return at our cost, cancelling your subscription.

5. **Free Monthly Newsletter!** It's the indispensable insiders' look at our most popular writers and their upcoming novels. Now you can have a behind-the-scenes look at the fascinating world of Silhouette! It's an added bonus you'll look forward to every month!

6. **More Surprise Gifts!** Because our home subscribers are our most valued readers, we'll be sending you additional free gifts from time to time — as a token of our appreciation.

FREE! 20k GOLD ELECTROPLATED CHAIN!

You'll love this 20k gold electroplated chain! The necklace is finely crafted with 160 double-soldered links, and is electroplate finished in genuine 20k gold. It's nearly 1/8" wide, fully 20" long — and has the look and feel of the real thing. "Glamorous" is the perfect word for it, and it can be yours FREE in this amazing Silhouette celebration!

SILHOUETTE ROMANCE™
FREE OFFER CARD

4 FREE BOOKS

20k GOLD ELECTROPLATED CHAIN—FREE

FREE MYSTERY BONUS

PLACE YOUR BALLOON STICKER HERE!

CONVENIENT HOME DELIVERY

FREE FACT-FILLED NEWSLETTER

MORE SURPRISE GIFTS THROUGHOUT THE YEAR—FREE

YES! Please send me my four Silhouette Romance™ novels FREE, along with my 20k Electroplated Gold Chain and my free mystery gift, as explained on the opposite page. I understand that accepting these books and gifts places me under no obligation ever to buy any books. I may cancel at any time for any reason, and the free books and gifts will be mine to keep!

315 CIS 815X

NAME
(PLEASE PRINT)

ADDRESS   APT

CITY   PROV

POSTAL CODE

SILHOUETTE "NO RISK GUARANTEE"
- There's no obligation to buy — the free books and gifts remain yours to keep.
- You receive books before they're available in stores.
- You may end your subscription anytime — just by letting us know.

PRINTED IN U.S.A.

feet in front of the man, for heaven's sake, and if their paths ever crossed in the future, she would be hard-pressed to come up with an excuse for having snubbed him so blatantly.

Managing a stiff smile, Shannon stood and straightened her shoulders. "I'm Shannon Doherty," she announced, extending her hand in what she hoped was a dignified manner. "I'm pleased to meet you, Mr. Wheeler."

Ross's gaze was as chilling as a north wind. Shannon saw that his eyes weren't the warm amber color of Mitch's; rather, they were a pale gray-blue—winter eyes that matched his voice.

He acknowledged her. "Ms. Doherty. Is there somewhere we could talk?"

Not one to waste time with the social amenities, Shannon thought sourly as she led him into her office. "Please have a seat, Mr. Wheeler." Shannon pointed to the chair across from her desk rather than the sofa. Somehow she wanted some distance between herself and this cool-eyed man. She also felt that sitting behind her desk would give herself some measure of control.

"I've been looking forward to meeting you, Ms. Doherty," Ross said, although his expression said otherwise. "Mitchell has spoken of you often." Careful words, spoken with authority. "He very much appreciates the manner in which you've assisted with the children. It's given him a much-needed break."

Shannon felt as though she'd been doused with ice water. Assisted with the children? She forced her expression to remain blank. Ross had paused and was watching her closely.

"They are adorable children." Her voice was calm and hardly shook at all. "I'm very fond of them...and of Mitch."

"Our family appreciates your concern." Ross's emphasis was placed to clearly separate Shannon from the Wheelers. "As you are no doubt aware, Mitchell has been under a tremendous strain since Kevin died. We've been after him to hire a housekeeper for the children, but he's refused."

Ross smiled for effect. "Mitchell has the rather quaint notion that hired help will cause some kind of psychological trauma to the children. It's rubbish, of course, but he's quite old-fashioned in many ways."

Ross leaned back in the chair, placing his elbows on the armrests and steepling his fingers. He watched Shannon as though evaluating the effect of his words. Shannon met his direct gaze, trying to conceal her turmoil.

"Please forgive my candor, Ms. Doherty, but I've been concerned about Mitchell for some time now."

Shannon clasped her fingers together and laid her knotted hands on the desk. "Concerned?"

"Yes. He hasn't been himself lately."

"Himself?" Shannon winced, knowing that she must sound like a confused parrot, yet was still unable to fully grasp the implication of Ross's words. Instinctively, however, she felt that those words would have a profound effect on her—and on her growing relationship with Mitch.

Licking her dry lips, Shannon opted for direct confrontation. "Mr. Wheeler, I not only forgive your candor, I insist upon it. If you've come here to say something specific, please do so."

There was a flicker of surprise in Ross's eyes and grudging respect. "Very well. As you're no doubt aware, my brother is a romantic. His views of the world, although laudable, are illusory and rather unrealistic. To understand his idealistic nature, one must delve into its origin. Are you prepared to do that?" He paused, awaiting her answer.

"Please continue." Did that tiny voice belong to her?

"Mitchell was just sixteen when our parents died and the years have distorted his childhood memories of their relationship. Incidents that don't conform to his image of perfection have been conveniently suppressed."

"I don't understand what this could possibly have to do with me or—"

"If I could impose upon your patience for a few moments longer, I believe the relevance will be established." Arching an eyebrow, Ross waited until Shannon sighed and motioned him to continue. "Now that Mitchell has taken the responsibility of raising Kevin's children, he seems to feel the necessity of recreating this image of domestic bliss. Admirable, of course, but not realistic."

Bewildered, Shannon helplessly shook her head. "Why have you told me this?"

Ross's expression softened and as his eyes warmed briefly, Shannon saw compassion and perhaps regret. The moment was fleeting, quickly replaced by an icy calm. "That should be obvious. Although Mitchell wouldn't consciously exploit your, ah, friendship, the stress he's endured may have clouded his perceptions."

"A-are you trying to say that Mitch has been using me?"

"Not intentionally, of course, but as I've mentioned, Mitchell has not been himself."

He paused again, offering Shannon the opportunity to respond. She ignored it, too stunned to speak. Ross couldn't know the pain his words had wrought. Ross was subtly suggesting that Shannon was being used as a child-care convenience, a role she'd played once before, with tragic results. All the fears, the niggling doubts that had been gnawing at her, suddenly bubbled to the surface.

Smoothly, Ross continued. "The family members all feel quite badly about the way in which you were, shall we say, thrust into this situation with the children's grandparents. Certainly you mustn't feel as though you have any culpability in the matter."

"'Culpability'?"

Ross flicked his hand casually. "I'm sure that your kindness toward Mitch and the children has nothing to do with the original incident. After all, you have nothing to make up for."

"What?" Shannon stood, unable to believe Ross's implication. Was he now suggesting that she was seeing Mitch to work out some kind of guilt trip?

"I've upset you. My apologies." Ross pushed back the chair and straightened. "I felt that under the circumstances, this discussion was necessary."

"Mr. Wheeler, I have absolutely no idea what those circumstances are." Shannon's eyes narrowed. "Did Mitch send you?"

"Not at all. In fact, it would be best if he remained unaware of our little visit."

Shannon spoke through clamped teeth. "Best for whom?"

Ross's smile was lazy but his eyes held a warning. "Best for both of us, Ms. Doherty. Good day." With that, he turned and strode from the room.

Lindsay slipped through the doorway, took one look at Shannon and froze. "You're pale as a bed sheet. What on earth is wrong?"

In low, clipped tones, Shannon told her.

"Heavy-duty," Lindsay murmured.

"What if he's right?"

Lindsay regarded her friend in silence for a moment. "I don't believe that. But from what you've told me, I do believe he's a very cynical and very unhappy man." She sighed and looked toward the doorway through which Ross Wheeler had disappeared, then added, "What a waste."

THE ADVENTURES OF BIFF BARNETT,
PRIVATE INVESTIGATOR

As Maggie pours two cups of coffee, Biff looks out her office window and sees a smiling couple pushing a baby carriage. Biff says, "You ever think about having kids, Maggie?"

Surprised, Maggie hands Biff a cup. "Sure. Someday."

Still staring out the window, Biff watches a laughing couple stroll by, arm in arm, obviously in love.

Biff sighs. "Ever get lonely?"

Eyeing him skeptically, Maggie says, "Everyone gets lonely, Barnett."

"Yeah, but you're not getting any younger, Maggie." Biff turns back to the window. "I mean, have you ever thought about trading your badge for an apron?"

Maggie chokes on her coffee.

Ten minutes to seven, which was five minutes later than the last time Shannon had looked at the clock. Nervously she stared into the mirror and fingered her opera-length faux pearls. Maybe she should have worn her black chiffon. Were those circles under her eyes? She found her makeup tube, then squinted critically at her reflection. If she used any more of this stuff, it would cake her face like a death mask. She dropped the tube on the dresser.

Too much eye shadow, she decided. That was the problem. Grabbing a tissue, she scoured her eyelids, then examined the results. Great. Now she resembled a red-eyed panda. And why was her hair sticking up like that?

Moaning, she turned away and began to pace. Pacing was good. Useless, but it gave her feet something to do. Now, if only she could occupy her mind.

Tonight was special. Shannon knew instinctively that this evening would herald, for better or for worse, a dramatic change in her relationship with Mitch. Lindsay had told her to go with the flow and let nature take its course, but what if nature ran amok? Shannon knew that her dearest friend felt that a roaring affair would be just what the doctor ordered to bring the bloom back to Shannon's cheeks. Heaven knows, Mitch Wheeler certainly made her hormones vibrate.

Still, such a change in their relationship would constitute a very serious step for Shannon—a step she'd never taken before. There was something special about Mitch and about Shannon's feelings for him. She'd always assumed that she had loved her ex-husband, but what she'd felt for Robert Willis paled in comparison to this new, almost frightening emotion. Her feelings for Mitch were deeply intense yet tenderly sweet.

But what was Mitch feeling? Shannon wondered. There was also the matter of Ross Wheeler's upsetting visit this afternoon. Mitch's older brother was an enigma, and Shannon had yet to figure his motive. One niggling thought kept seeping into her mind. What if Ross was right? What if he was actually giving her a direct and honest warning? It was a thought Shannon couldn't bear to examine.

The doorbell rang. It was show time.

Mitch Wheeler stood in the hallway outside Shannon's apartment, and for the fifth time, patted the bulge in his breast pocket. He hadn't been this nervous since his pet lizard had escaped during Sunday school.

Maybe he should have let Shannon pick out the ring. It was only a diamond. Maybe he should have bought her emeralds. Redheads looked wonderful in emeralds. Maybe—

The door swung open and Mitch's breath caught in his throat. Shannon had never looked more beautiful. She wore a long-sleeved sheath of dark green satin that draped every curve of her body. Her elegance was enhanced by simple pearl earrings and a matching necklace.

"You—you look wonderful," Mitch said hoarsely, wondering how he would be able to keep his hands off her.

"Thank you. So do you." Her gaze slid approvingly over his formal evening suit.

Mitch's mouth went dry. They stared at each other, the rest of the world forgotten.

Shannon blinked, as though awakening. "I'm so sorry. Please, come in." She closed the door behind him. "Would you like something to drink? I have some white wine and I think I have some brandy."

"Nothing, thanks." He tugged at his collar. "You look wonderful."

Shannon's smile was slow and very female. "Thank you."

"I, uh, already said that, didn't I?"

Her laugh was husky. "I never tire of hearing it."

"I'll never tire of telling you."

" 'Never' is a long time," she murmured, suddenly shy.

Mitch saw the pink glow on her cheeks. He was charmed by how easily she blushed.

Abruptly she changed the subject. "Where are the children?"

"Ross is staying with them."

Mitch noticed Shannon's fleeting frown and wondered about it.

"You and Ross are very close, aren't you?" she asked.

"Yes, I guess we are. Actually, we've always been a pretty tight-knit family."

"Does the rest of your family live nearby?"

"Yes, the entire Wheeler clan is located in Los Angeles County," Mitch said. "My older sister, JoAnn, lives about ten miles away. She's happily married with two great kids of her own. My younger sister, Lauren, is a CPA in Thousand Oaks. Joshua is a marketing rep for a large computer company downtown and Ross has a condo a couple of miles from the house. His law office is here in Pasadena."

Shannon cleared her throat and stretched her lips into a tense smile. "So, Ross is the oldest?"

Nodding, Mitch said, "Yes, so he's always had the lion's share of responsibility for the rest of us and he takes it very seriously."

"He certainly does—I mean, I can see that he would— take his responsibility seriously, that is." The frown furrowed deeper, then disappeared. "Now, are you going to tell me where we're going tonight, or do I have to wear a blindfold until we get there?"

Mitch's eyes sparkled as he reached into his pocket, pulled out two tickets and held them in front of her.

Shannon's eyes widened. "*Les Misérables*? That's been sold-out for weeks."

"My agent pulled a couple of strings and the curtain goes up in thirty minutes." He cupped his palm against her back. "Shall we go?"

* * *

The lobby of the Shubert Theater was dazzling, a collage of sparkling crystal and beautiful people. Shannon had an uncomfortable sense of déjà vu. Her husband had frequented such events, along with charity balls, political fundraisers and other "who's who" functions appropriate for a man of his financial stature. Shannon had hated it all. She had despised the pomposity and arrogance of Robert's social circle, vowing never to accept superficiality over substance.

But here she was, clinging to Mitch's arm as though he were her life raft in a sea of glitz. Flashbulbs popped, microphones were shoved into tightly woven groups of people in the hope that someone of importance was saying something profound, and reporters buzzed like insects on spoiled fruit.

A raven-haired beauty whom Shannon vaguely recognized as a popular television actress regally responded to rapidly hurled questions.

"Any truth to the rumor that your series is going to be canceled next season . . . ?"

"We hear your marriage is on the rocks. Care to comment . . . ?"

"Have you started work on a new film . . . ?"

"How about a big smile for the camera?—that's great."

The woman handled herself with admirable aplomb, Shannon thought. Shannon personally felt claustrophobic when surrounded by such a seething wall of flesh. Of course, she'd only been the center of attention during that horrible incident with Trudy, and the siege of questions had little to do with business. The reporters had circled like starving sharks whipped into a feeding frenzy by the scent of scandal.

She began to tremble. The flashbulbs, curtly barked questions, microphones—Shannon's mind was soon lost in the past.

Suddenly there was a blinding flash of light. Reflexively, Shannon's hand shielded her eyes and she felt Mitch pull her closer. A disheveled scarecrow of a man with owlish eyes and an immense Adam's apple blocked their path.

"Mr. Wheeler? Rob Hall, *Valley Gazette*." The man let his camera dangle from his neck and whipped out a writing pad. He squinted at Shannon. "Aren't you that model from the cover of *Fashion Universe*?"

Shannon managed to stammer that she wasn't. Disappointed, Hall turned back to Mitch.

"My readers have wondered where you've been keeping yourself, Mr. Wheeler." His elbow connected with Mitch's rib cage. "Hey, how about a little inside info on Bill's latest story line."

Mitch's smile was stiff. "Now, Rob, you know that's top-secret stuff. Your readers will just have to wait, like everyone else."

The lobby lights dimmed briefly. Five minutes until first curtain. Looking relieved, Mitch politely ushered Shannon into the theater.

"Sorry about that," Mitch whispered after they were seated. "Hollywood public-relations people send their clients to these events and then leak the news to the media hoping for a little free publicity. We just got caught in the cross fire." Mitch lifted her hand to his lips. "Shannon? Honey, you're shaking."

"It's nothing." She forced a smile. "Too much excitement, I guess." She paused, then said, "Mitch, that man took our picture."

"Lucky devil. You look gorgeous tonight."

"Is it—is it going to be in the newspaper?"

"What?"

"The picture."

"I don't know. It depends on whether they need to fill space."

Shannon could almost visualize the results if that picture were published. Someone out there, someone with the memory of an elephant and the tenacity of a bulldog would recognize her. An old scandal with a celebrity twist could turn her life and Mitch's into another media circus. The idea might thrill Mitch's PR man, but it definitely did *not* thrill Shannon.

"I don't want them to use that picture."

Something in her desperate tone caught Mitch's attention. "Why not? Why are you so upset?"

"I—I'm just a rather private person, that's all. Can't you stop them? Please?"

"Okay, honey. Okay." Mitch's voice was soothing. "I'll take care of it."

Shannon's muscles went limp with relief. "Thank you."

Still, she argued with herself over her panicky reaction. She'd known since day one that Mitch Wheeler was news, yet she'd chosen to be with him. Certainly she was intelligent enough to realize that sooner or later, their friendship would be duly noted by those who reported such things.

Why was she behaving like a frightened wimp? Mitch was with her. Everything was fine. No, it was better than fine, it was wonderful. The past was over, she told herself firmly. She had no need to be afraid of flashbulbs and reporters. It was Mitch they were interested in, not her.

She pushed away the niggling doubts and tried to ignore her discomfort. Already she regretted expressing concern about the photographs. This was Mitch's world, and for some reason Shannon didn't understand, it was important that he not realize how ill-equipped she was to cope with it.

"Are you sure you're all right?" Mitch whispered.

"Yes." She attempted to punctuate her answer with a smile. "I'm fine."

Mitch, seeming unconvinced by her weak assurance, rested his palm against her cheek. "Do you want to leave?"

"No. I'm right where I want to be. With you." Turning her head, Shannon kissed his hand. She heard Mitch's sharp intake of breath and felt his arm tremble.

As the theater sank into darkness, Shannon was aware only of the man beside her. His body heat seemed to scorch her, his sweet, spicy scent enveloped her. A light shone from the stage, a blur of color and motion. Music echoed around them. She was aware, but unable to concentrate. To her, it was melody without structure, lyrics without form.

At first Shannon forced her eyes forward, feigning interest in the performance. Mitch's nearness overwhelmed her. Every nuance of her mind was attuned to him, to the feel of his warm hand covering hers, to the rhythm of his breathing. His scent mingled with hers, creating a musky aura that belonged to neither alone, but was uniquely their own.

Finally, she gave in to the need to look at him and found his gaze locked upon her. The planes of his face were sculpted by the moodlighting of the play, which changed with the scenes from hot amber to somber blues. Shannon watched Mitch, fascinated, oblivious to the activity onstage. He held her captive with his eyes. He stroked her wrist with his fingertip—feathering strokes that sensitized and aroused.

She was trembling again, but not in fear.

Suddenly a dark silence fell over the theater, then the lights brightened. The vibration of music turned to the drone of shuffling feet and humming conversation. Intermission.

They sat as though glued to their seats, minds melded, eyes focused only on each other. Finally Mitch blinked and looked around, seeming surprised by his surroundings. On the armrest between them, their hands were so tightly intertwined that a casual observer would have difficulty noting where one ended and another began.

"Are you, ah, enjoying the play?" Mitch's voice was strained.

"Umm? Oh, yes. Very much." What play? Shannon's foggy brain asked.

"Good." Mitch looked sheepish. "Could you tell me what it's about?"

"Actually, I haven't a clue."

He chuckled softly. "I'm sorry. I wanted this to be such a special evening for you."

"It is," Shannon said in a sultry whisper.

Mitch's slow, sexy smile melted her. "We have reservations for dinner after the show, but I can cancel them if you like."

"I'd like that very much."

Shannon felt Mitch's hands tighten convulsively. She saw his eyes turned smoky, then he whispered, "Let's go."

Shakily she managed to stand and turn toward the aisle. Mitch was behind her, with his hands caressing her shoulders and the heat of his hard chest burning into her back. When she felt his lips brush the nape of her neck, her knees turned to soup.

Somehow they managed to get out of the theater under their own power. Mitch steered the car onto the freeway and pulled Shannon as close as she could get without sitting on his lap. He glanced at her as frequently as the traffic would allow, seeming to reassure himself that she was still beside him. His eyes glowed with a soft reverence, as though he were observing a priceless work of art.

And Shannon felt priceless. She felt cherished and wanted and beautiful. She didn't speak, she didn't think. She simply allowed herself to feel.

Even when Mitch had to return his attention to the road, Shannon watched him, memorizing the lift of his straight brow, the small crease in his cheek. Then she noticed that he seemed a bit pale. His forehead was damp and he frequently patted his breast pocket. Was he nervous? she wondered, then dismissed the thought. Shannon didn't even want to think about nerves or she would personally go into an anxiety spasm.

When Mitch drove into the parking structure of her apartment complex, Shannon wasn't at all surprised. By the time they got off the elevator in front of her door, however, her sensual high had been battered by the resurgence of her rational mind.

She walked stiffly. What was she doing? Never mind that. Shannon knew *what* she was doing, but her brain was frantically trying to sort out *why*. She kept seeing Ross's chilling gaze, kept hearing his hurtful words: *Mitchell hasn't been himself lately*.

Mitch pried the key from her fingers and opened the door. He was ashen. Beads of perspiration dotted his upper lip.

Once inside, they shuffled like insecure adolescents and carried on a stilted, monosyllabic conversation.

Shannon's attempt at a bright smile ended when her lips stuck to her teeth. "Coffee?" She was pouring water into the coffee maker before she heard Mitch's affirmative reply.

Continuing to putter in the kitchen while the coffee dripped, Shannon angled a glance over the breakfast counter and saw Mitch wandering about her living room like a lost soul. He picked up a magazine, idly flipped the pages, then dropped it back into the rack. He patted his pocket again. He studied the pile of textbooks strewn across her dining-room table. Finally, he walked over to read the cross-stitched sampler that hung over her desk and said: Plumbers Have Pipe Dreams.

"Did you make this?" he asked, pointing to the wall hanging.

"No, but I made the desk."

"You're kidding." Mitch ran his hand over the polished cherry surface. He smiled, remembered how beautifully Snyder's doghouse had turned out. "No, I guess you're not kidding."

Shannon set two steaming mugs on the coffee table. "I'm sorry I don't have any good china...." Her voice trailed off as Mitch stood mere inches in front of her. Automatically her head tilted back and her lips parted.

"Thank you," Mitch whispered raggedly.

"For what?"

"Coffee."

"Oh."

Her tongue darted out to moisten her lips. "Perhaps we should sit down."

"Of course," he said, but remained firmly planted where he stood. Mitch lifted one finger and traced the delicate curves of her face. He opened his mouth to speak, but only a contented sigh emerged as he slid his finger under Shannon's chin, gently lifting until she looked him straight in the eye. "Shannon, I..." His words rolled into a moan as he circled her waist with his free hand and pulled her against him.

Then his lips were on her throat, her cheeks, her eyelids. He was speaking small, mumbled words against her skin. She couldn't hear them but they inflamed her. Again, their scents mingled and filled the warm night air with an intimate, passionate perfume. She thrust her fingers into his hair and pulled his lips closer, taking his whispered words into her mouth.

Her heart seemed to swell inside her breast, beating until she feared it would explode. Now she knew *why* she was here and why Mitch was with her. It was because she was in love with him, more deeply than she had ever loved another. It was because there was no place in the world she wanted to be at this moment, except in his arms. It wasn't logical, it might not even be wise, but it was indisputable.

She wouldn't let herself think about Mitch's other world, his world of glamour, the world to which she could never really belong. She pushed Ross's warning from her mind. It was *this* man who mattered. It was Mitch.

Gasping for breath, holding each other as though to stop the room from spinning, they ended the kiss.

"Shannon, you're so special," Mitch murmured. "What I feel for you, what you do to me, it's all so new, so different." He slid his palms to her cheeks, cupping her face tenderly, flicking a damp streak from under her eyes with his thumb. "Tears? Have I hurt you?"

"No. Oh, no." She closed her eyes. "It's just so sweet. Incredibly sweet. I feel—" She stopped, shaking her head, unable to complete the sentence.

"Then let me tell you how I feel." Mitch's voice shook and he swallowed to steady it. "I need you, Shannon. I—I—What on earth is that noise?"

Blinking, Shannon's gaze flickered toward the obnoxious buzzing sound. "The telephone, I think."

Reluctantly, Mitch released his grip and allowed her to answer the phone. He took several deep breaths and tried to calm his shaking hands.

Everything was going as planned—no, it was going even better than planned. He couldn't have imagined the sweet softness of her body melting against his, how her eyes had filled with wonder when he'd kissed her.

As soon as she returned, Mitch knew that he would slip the ring on her finger and ask her to spend the rest of her life with him. Then the entire world would open before them and his dreams—their dreams—would come true.

A perfect family, a perfect life.

Suddenly, Mitch felt cold. Something was wrong, terribly wrong. Whirling, he looked directly into Shannon's horrified face.

"Mitch?" Shannon's voice sounded hollow. "It's your brother, Ross. There's been an emergency." The words seemed to choke her. "I-it's Rachel."

Chapter Seven

Mitch jammed his thumb on the elevator button for the third time. "Come on," he muttered, then turned to Shannon. "Where are the stairs?"

"At the other end of the hall, but we're on the sixth floor." She laid her hand on his arm and started to say something else, but was interrupted as the elevator door whooshed open.

They stepped in. Mitch stuffed his hands in his pockets and stared at the flashing numbers that signaled their descent.

"Exactly what did Ross say?" Shannon asked.

"Umm?" Mitch blinked at her. "Oh. He said that Rachel was running a fever and was sick to her stomach."

Shannon chewed her lower lip, then said, "Maybe it's just a virus."

"Maybe." Mitch was unconvinced. Ross wasn't the type to overreact and Mitch was certain he wouldn't have called unless he had good reason.

The elevator slowed, then stopped. An elderly couple stepped in, smiling a polite greeting. Shannon returned their smile, nodding an acknowledgement. Mitch rocked impatiently on his heels, again staring at the numbers over the door.

Finally, they reached the garage and hurried to Mitch's car. As he slipped the key into the ignition, he glanced gratefully at Shannon. The evening was turning into a disaster, but she was a real trooper. She'd insisted on returning to the house with him, saying that she wouldn't sleep a wink until she knew Rachel was all right.

"Shannon, I'm sorry—"

She stopped his words by placing a finger on his lips. Mitch's heart thumped at her touch.

"I understand," she said. "Please, let's hurry."

Swallowing, Mitch nodded and twisted the key. As the engine roared to life, he quickly backed the car out of its parking space. The underground garage was a large structure, complex and multileveled. Mentally reversing the route he'd taken earlier that evening, Mitch shoved the car into gear and stepped on the gas.

As he drove down the dimly lit ramp toward the exit, Mitch's mind wandered. Before the telephone had rung, he'd had his hand on the ring and the words on his tongue. It had taken all his courage but he'd looked into those spring-green eyes and known, without doubt, that this was *the* woman for him.

Would she have agreed to marry him? he wondered. Or would she have refused? No, she wouldn't have refused. She loved the kids and wanted a family as much as he did.

"Mitch!"

Startled, he looked over at Shannon. Her eyes were wide and she was pointing straight ahead. "This is the wrong way!"

Jerking his head around, he saw that the driveway forked ahead and he was speeding toward the entrance instead of the exit.

Before his foot could hit the brake, the car lurched once and there was a sharp ripping sound, a deafening bang and a loud shudder. The steering wheel went rigid, as though suddenly welded in place and Mitch fought desperately to steer the limping car to a stop.

Shocked, Mitch and Shannon stared at each other. "Are you all right?" he asked.

She managed to nod, then they scrambled from the car to assess the damage.

Mitch moaned. The one-way entrance road had been guarded by a long metal rake jutting from the concrete. Tooth-like prongs, which collapsed harmlessly when approached from the proper direction, had attacked like giant, tire-eating piranhas.

Shaking his head, he gestured helplessly toward the four shredded rubber lumps and looked at Shannon. He saw compassion in her eyes and felt a wave of humiliation. "I—I can't believe I did that."

"It could have happened to anyone." Shannon's voice took on a teasing tone. "Even Biff Barnett."

Mitch stared bleakly at the car.

Sighing, Shannon asked, "Can you drive it to that curb so it doesn't block the driveway?"

Following her gaze, Mitch saw the appointed place and nodded.

Shannon reached into the front seat, grabbed her purse, then headed back into the garage. By the time Mitch had coaxed the wounded car the additional twenty feet, Shannon had pulled up beside him, rolled down the window of her tiny compact car and flashed him a bright smile. "Going my way?"

"Always," Mitch murmured and folded himself into the passenger seat.

Fifteen minutes later, they arrived and hurried into the house. Shannon saw Ross appear at the top of the balustrade, hesitate briefly, then start down the stairs.

Mitch met him halfway. "How is she?"

Ross answered, but spoke so quietly that Shannon couldn't hear his response. She saw Mitch nod. Then, without a backward glance at Shannon, he sprinted up the remaining steps and disappeared down the hallway.

Turning, Ross looked down and met Shannon's direct gaze. "I'm sorry to have spoiled your evening, Ms. Doherty."

Somehow Shannon doubted that. She'd seen a glint of surprise in Ross's eyes, as though he hadn't expected her to return with Mitch. Keeping a carefully neutral expression, she said. "You didn't. May I see Rachel now?"

"Yes, of course." Ross stepped back to allow Shannon access to the stairs. As she passed him, he fell into step behind her. "I hope you'll forgive my brother's lapse in manners," he said, apparently referring to Mitch's abandoning Shannon in the entry. "He doesn't mean to be thoughtless, but the children do tend to be the center of his focus."

Shannon felt a slow heat rising and wondered if the entire incident had been a carefully orchestrated demonstration. "I understand."

Ross stepped in front of Shannon, blocking the door to Rachel's bedroom. "I'm happy to hear that," he said quietly, then stood aside as Shannon entered the room.

Her suspicions dissipated instantly. There was Rachel, tiny and pale, pitifully curled on a too-large mattress. Shannon tried to swallow a gasp of dismay, but her throat seemed to have closed up, squeezed by some invisible hand. Her heart literally throbbed at the sight.

A bowl of water was on the nightstand and Mitch, sitting on the bed, was tenderly sponging Rachel's forehead.

"Oh, Mitch," Shannon whispered. "She's so... so little and she looks so sick."

At the sound of Shannon's voice, Mitch turned and Rachel forced her eyelids open. She managed a weak smile and said, "Hi."

Shannon went to her. "Hi, honey. How are you feeling?"

"My neck hurts." She pointed to her throat with one pudgy finger. "Uncle Ross says I have a fleever."

"Fever, pumpkin," Mitch corrected, then appeared suddenly startled and looked from Shannon to Ross. "I'm sorry, I forgot that you two hadn't met."

"We took the liberty of handling our own introductions," Ross said smoothly.

"Good." Mitch's attention returned to Rachel and he touched her pink cheek. "Did you take her temperature, Ross?"

Ross nodded. "A hundred and one. I gave her two children's aspirin—" he glanced at his watch "—about an hour ago."

Shannon wrung her hands. As a child, she herself had been exceptionally healthy, remembering only a few sniffles and a bout with chicken pox. Nor, thankfully, could she ever remember her stepdaughter being ill, so seeing Rachel like this was a frightening experience.

Shannon felt helpless and ignorant. "Should we take her to the hospital?"

Rachel's eyes rounded. "I don't like hospitals."

"Shh, honey. Let's just take a look, okay?" As Mitch coaxed Rachel to open her mouth, Shannon backed away, watching with increasing awe. Rachel was looking up with big, trusting eyes as Mitch took charge, examining the child with a competence born of obvious experience. Murmuring soft encouragement, Mitch's fingers gently probed the back of her neck, then lightly massaged beneath her jaw.

The area was apparently sore. Rachel protested and Mitch soothed her, brushing damp strands of hair from her face and whispering softly. Finally, he said, "I think what we have here is another case of tonsillitis."

Shannon blinked. "How do you know that?"

"I don't for certain, but she had tonsillitis about three months ago and the symptoms are the same. See this swelling?" Mitch pointed to some puffiness on the side of Rachel's neck. "My hunch is that by the time we get to the doctor's office tomorrow, she's going to look like an overgrown chipmunk."

Mitch tweaked her snubbed nose and Rachel giggled, nestling into the puffy pillows.

As Mitch bent to kiss Rachel's forehead, Shannon was touched by his tenderness with the child but she also felt like an intruder.

Turning, she quietly left the room and went downstairs.

Her mind replayed the evening's events. She remembered the soft power of Mitch's lips against hers and how his hands had stoked flames of passion beyond her experience, beyond even her wildest fantasies.

She had wanted him, needed him, and as passion mingled with fear, she had realized that she'd fallen in love with him. If Ross hadn't called, Shannon knew that there would probably have been a major change in their relationship—a physical change, a spiritual change.

They would have made love.

For Shannon, such intimacy represented an emotional bonding, a commitment for the future. But what would it have represented to Mitch? She now knew Mitch wasn't a superficial person, and Ross's grim opinion to the contrary, Shannon was convinced that Mitch truly cared for her.

Shannon desperately needed time to think, time to sort out her feelings. Mitch Wheeler represented everything she'd ever wanted—a gentle, loving man, a beautiful family. But he also represented everything she feared—parallels of a past that still haunted her. For six years, Shannon had cultivated a career, pursued an education and established control of her own life. It was a full life, a safe life, but until she'd met Mitch, Shannon realized that it was also a lonely one.

What she felt for Mitch—the way her chest ached when she looked at him, the way her throat tightened when he touched her—these feelings went far beyond mere caring. And that frightened her.

She didn't want to be hurt again. Shannon had lessons to remember, lessons from the past.

"Shannon?"

Startled, she whirled and saw Mitch come into the living room. She managed a nervous smile, hoping the direction of her thoughts hadn't been visibly etched on her face. "How's Rachel?"

"She's asleep for the moment. Her fever's down a bit." He raked at his hair. "Shannon, about tonight—"

Shannon interrupted. "How long does tonsillitis usually last?"

"Umm? Oh, that depends. The doctor will probably prescribe some antibiotics and eventually the tonsils will have to come out."

Wincing at the thought, Shannon turned away. "How awful."

Mitch shrugged. "It's not so bad. When I had my tonsils out, I got all the ice cream and soda I wanted. In fact, anytime I wanted attention I'd grab my throat, fall to the ground and croak, 'Ice cream.'"

Shannon laughed. "Manipulative little devil, weren't you?"

"Well, it worked for a while. Then they got wise to me." Mitch's expression turned serious and Shannon saw him pat his jacket again. This time, she noticed a bulge, as though something lumpy had been stuffed into the breast pocket. He cleared his throat. "Ah, before Ross called, I was trying to say something."

Mitch's mouth went dry. He'd never done this before and the words seemed to stick on his tongue. Shannon's head was tilted, her eyes clear and questioning. She was so beautiful.

As though he couldn't help himself, he touched her face, stroking the soft skin of her cheek with his thumb. "I've been thinking about, er, things. That is, I've been thinking about you." He paused, but she made no comment and he forged ahead. "You've become a very special part of my life, Shannon. The kids love you and you seem to love them too, but, well, I've been thinking that we should, ah, change our relationship."

He saw her eyes cloud with confusion as a tiny frown marred her brow. "I don't understand," she said quietly. "Would you rather we . . . didn't see each other?"

"No!" Mitch was aghast. "I want to see *more* of you. What we shared tonight—that is, almost shared..." His voice dissipated into a muffled moan.

Shannon's eyes narrowed skeptically and Mitch felt his neck heat. Obviously, this was coming across as more of a proposition than a proposal and he was chagrined by his lack of finesse. He started to explain that his intentions were purely honorable, then snapped his mouth shut. Words had gotten him into this mess. Actions, he decided, would be best.

Slipping his hand into his jacket, he fumbled in the pocket and closed his hand around the small velvet box. "Shannon, I—"

Ross strode into the room. "I'll call the towing service and..." Ross's voice trailed off and he seemed to realize that he'd interrupted something delicate. To confirm that fact, Mitch shot him a look of pure frustration. "Ah, I beg your pardon," Ross said, then discreetly left them alone.

The mood, however, had been broken.

Shannon, looking extremely uncomfortable, managed a strained smile. "I should be going now."

"Wait." Mitch's hand closed over her shoulder. He couldn't simply let her leave thinking, well, whatever it was that she was probably thinking. "I have something to ask you," he finally blurted.

Her eyebrow lifted. "Oh?"

"Yes. I—" Mitch saw Ross peek into the room, holding a telephone receiver.

"Forgive the intrusion but the tow-truck driver wants the license number of your car."

"Oh, for pity's sake, I don't have it memorized. Why does he need it?"

Ross shrugged. "So he won't tow the wrong vehicle, I assume."

Aggravated, Mitch spoke through clamped teeth. "Tell him it's the only car on the block with four flat tires."

Ross got the message. "Right," he mumbled, then disappeared.

When Mitch turned back to Shannon, he saw that she was digging car keys out of her purse. "It's late and I have an early field job tomorrow. I really should be going."

Defeated, Mitch slipped the box back into his pocket and said, "Will I see you tomorrow?"

She looked at him for a long time, and suddenly Mitch was afraid of her answer. After what seemed like an eternity, she smiled. "I'll stop by after work to see Rachel."

"And to see me, too, I hope."

Lowering her eyes, she murmured, "Of course."

Her shy gesture touched Mitch and he felt ten feet tall. Tomorrow, then, would be the night. He would propose and she'd accept and everything in the world would be wonderful. His voice was husky. "Tomorrow then. Meanwhile, Ross will see that you get home safely tonight."

Shannon blinked in surprise. "I don't need a ride. My car's right outside."

"Since it's on his way home, Ross is going to meet the tow truck in front of your apartment building. I asked him to follow you home." Seeing her indignant expression, Mitch lifted her chin and brushed his lips against her mouth. "I know it's old-fashioned, but won't you humor me? It's so late and I'd just feel better knowing you got home safe and sound."

Smiling, Shannon murmured, "I guess chivalry isn't dead, after all."

"Not where you're concerned." Mitch lifted her face, kissed her softly, then watched her walk into the night. He fought the engulfing emptiness, the sense of loss. Tomorrow, he told himself. Tomorrow would be the beginning of a new life—for all of them.

The following afternoon, Shannon pulled into Mitch's driveway, turned off the engine and with a weary moan, relaxed against the padded headrest. Lying awake until dawn had forced her to face a long, grueling day with red eyes and a foggy brain. Sleep was beginning to seem like a fond and distant memory, a comforting state that had eluded her for weeks. At work, she'd tried to keep her mind busy but at the weirdest possible moments she would suddenly visualize Mitch's face, or imagine the silky touch of his fingers on her cheek.

Being in love, Shannon decided, was simply not what it was cracked up to be.

Exactly *what* had Mitch been trying to tell her last night? By three in the morning, Shannon had been certain that he was going to break off their relationship completely and she'd primed herself to be brave—no tears, no recriminations, no blame laid.

At five o'clock, however, she'd remembered that Mitch had insisted that he wanted to see *more* of her. Exactly *how much* more was the question. What free time Shannon's hectic schedule allowed was already spent with Mitch. Did he want her to create more time by giving up school or eliminating Saturdays with Pop? Possibly. Mitch had made several half-teasing remarks to that effect.

By noon, however, Shannon had come to the conclusion that Mitch, too, had been considering the implications of a more personal relationship. After all, they were both adults living in a modern, liberated society.

But in spite of Lindsay's not-so-subtle prodding, Shannon realized that she was simply not the type for a casual affair. Making love with Mitch would be far from casual.

Rubbing her aching head, Shannon squeezed her eyelids shut and wondered with trepidation what the coming evening would bring. For better or worse, she sensed that the unfolding events would change her life.

Shannon forced herself to step from the car and walk shakily to the porch. She hesitated, then stiffened with determination and poked the doorbell.

The door swung open.

"Hi, Dusty," Shannon said. "How are you today?"

Dusty regarded her grumpily, then shrugged.

Shannon was instantly alarmed by the boy's behavior. "How's Rachel? She's all right, isn't she?"

Another shrug. "Yeah, I guess."

"Did she go to the doctor today?"

"Yeah." Dusty stood in the doorway, blocking her entrance. He eyed her warily, then stared at his own shoes.

"Is something wrong, Dusty?" Shannon was concerned. Dusty was usually a happy, outgoing boy. He was far from perfect, of course, and Shannon knew he could be sulky and petulant, unpleasant reminders of her stepdaughter. But she firmly reminded herself that Dusty was a child and one must expect childish behavior.

Lowering herself to the boy's height, Shannon asked, "Do you want to talk about it?" She ruffled his hair. "Now, 'fess up. What's the problem?"

Dusty glanced behind him, as though assuring himself that he couldn't be overheard, then said, "I'm hungry."

"What?" Startled, Shannon stepped in and closed the door behind her.

"It's past dinnertime and Uncle Mitch is still working," he grumbled.

"I see."

Dusty glared at the stairs. "Rachel got ice cream and soda pop and stuff, but I didn't get anything."

"Ah. Now I *really* see." Shannon tried to stifle her smile. Dusty's jealousy was understandable and his feelings should be considered. Lowering her voice, Shannon adopted a conspiratorial tone and whispered, "I'll see what I can do, okay?"

Dusty grinned. "Okay," he said, then hollered, "Shannon's here!" to no one in particular, and shot up the stairs.

Mitch came out of his office and when he saw Shannon, his expression warmed. Still, Shannon thought he looked tired and wondered if he, too, had spent a sleepless night.

He'd taken two steps toward her when the telephone rang and Mitch swore. "That's probably my agent again. Just because I'm still a bit behind, the man feels he has free license to drive me insane."

When Mitch had nearly reached his office door, he glanced over his shoulder with a grim expression. "Don't go away."

Startled by his commanding tone, Shannon could only mumble, "I won't."

Satisfied, Mitch disappeared through the doorway.

Shannon was still wondering about Mitch's abrupt change when she heard babyish babble. Following the sound, she found Stefie in the playpen. The toddler looked up, cooed happily, then stretched her fat arms up, pleading for release.

Unable to resist, Shannon scooped her up and gave the giggling baby a hug. "I'm happy to see you, too, Stefie," Shannon murmured.

Caesar the cat had been napping on the sofa. The animal seemed annoyed at the disturbance, and after stretching regally, he tossed Shannon a disdainful look.

"Kee ka!" Stefie chortled gleefully.

"Yes, sugar, it's a kitty cat."

As Stefie's fat hands clapped with delight, Shannon heard the office door slam, to be followed by forceful footsteps. Then Mitch marched into the living room. His expression was bleak.

"Problems?" she asked.

Looking exhausted and discouraged, Mitch rubbed his forehead. "My agent can't get the contract deadline extended. He says that New York wants the completed strips by noon tomorrow."

Shannon was worried, sadly noting that Mitch seemed to have aged in the past few weeks. His cheeks were drawn and stress lines creased his forehead.

"I've never had trouble keeping up before," Mitch muttered. "Story lines used to boil out of my brain on command. Now, every panel is a major struggle."

"You're trying to do too much, burning yourself out."

He shook his head. "I should be able to handle it."

"Handle what. Three full-time jobs as cartoonist, mother and father? Not to mention part-time cook, chauffeur, soccer coach.... Mitch, there are only twenty-four hours in the day." Shannon saw his mouth thin stubbornly. She softened her tone, hoping to reach him. "Why don't you simply get some help, Mitch. A housekeeper could—"

"No!"

Stunned by his vehemence, Shannon simply stared at him.

Mitch sighed, rubbing the back of his neck. "Look, honey, the kids need to be cared for by family, not strangers. Things are a little confused right now, but after we're—" He caught his breath. "I mean, it'll all work out."

Shannon thought he was being a bit idealistic and started to say so, but before Shannon could respond, Mitch glanced at his watch and moaned. "It can't be dinnertime already. I haven't even thawed anything."

He seemed so frustrated and forlorn, Shannon's insides turned to jelly. She longed to wrap her arms around him, to comfort and console and bring the twinkle back into his solemn eyes. Mitch had so much to deal with now, so much tension and responsibility. A high-stress job with constant deadlines was difficult enough, but adding Mitch's legal problems and the chaos of being a single parent to three small children—well, it was no wonder the man looked like a zombie.

Suddenly Shannon felt very small. Had she really thought Mitch had nothing better to do than lie awake worrying about their relationship? What ego!

Mustering her sweetest, most supportive smile, she said, "Not to worry, sir." Shannon shifted Stefie's weight to her hip and sauntered over to Mitch. "I'll take care of dinner. You sharpen your ink pens and go draw up a storm."

Mitch's face lit with relief, then his expression became wary. "You're not going to fix any of that frozen stuff, are you?"

Shannon's smile went rigid. That was exactly what she had planned to do. "Of course not. I have one or two items of culinary delight in my repertoire." Chili dogs. She could manage chili dogs.

"You're an angel." Mitch planted a quick kiss on her forehead and disappeared into his study.

The next two hours gave Shannon a whole new perspective on parenthood. She checked on Rachel, told Dusty that he was temporarily in charge, then grabbed Stefie and dashed to the grocery store. By the time she got back, it was nearly six-thirty and Dusty declared that he was almost starved to death. Shannon patted his head, told him to be brave and, after a brief moment of panic when she realized that there was no microwave, she threw a pound of hot dogs into the oven.

Dusty watched with interest. "How long will it take?"

"I'm not sure. How long does it take when Uncle Mitch makes them?"

"Uncle Mitch doesn't cook hot dogs. He hates 'em."

"Oh, that's just wonderful. Why didn't you tell me?"

Dusty fixed Shannon with a wide-eyed expression of total innocence. "You didn't ask."

"You haven't exactly been in a talkative mood."

Dusty's chin lowered to his chest. Shannon saw his lip quiver and quickly hugged him. "Never mind. You like hot dogs, don't you?"

A shrug. "Yeah."

"Well, then Uncle Mitch will just have to tough it out."

Dusty brightened. "Like when he makes me eat broccoli?"

"Umm, sort of." Shannon had been heating some chicken-noodle soup for Rachel and now poured it into a bowl. She added some bread and fruit and garnished the tray with a tiny pink rose from the yard. "I'm going to take this upstairs, then I'll tell Uncle Mitch that dinner's ready. Watch the chili for me, okay?"

"Okay."

Rachel was feeling well enough to enjoy every bit of the special attention she was receiving. When Shannon left, Rachel was happily slurping soup and watching cartoons on the small television Mitch had set up on the dresser.

Shannon was on the stairs when she heard Mitch's voice filtering from his study, low and angry. She noticed the study door was ajar and as she reached the doorway, she heard the telephone receiver being forcefully cradled. Tapping lightly on the door, she called Mitch's name.

His voice sound weary. "Come on in, honey."

"Is something wrong?"

Mitch rubbed his neck, then rolled his head as though trying to loosen his stiff muscles. His stretched smile was unconvincing. "Everything's fine."

Shannon regarded him skeptically. "Was that your agent again?"

"No, it was Ross."

Shannon tensed, then mentally scolded herself. Ross Wheeler was neither her problem nor her business. Still, Mitch was obviously upset by his brother's call and Shannon had a hunch as to the cause. "Has he heard from the Gilberts?"

Shannon saw Mitch's expression flicker, hardening briefly.

"It's nothing for you to worry about, just a bunch of legal mumbo-jumbo. Ross will take care of it." The tone of his voice was more commanding than hopeful, leaving no doubt that as far as Mitch was concerned, Ross had *better* take care of it.

Shannon slid her hand over Mitch's stiff shoulders. "What *is* going on with the Gilberts?"

"I've told you. They're still not convinced that I'm a fit guardian, that's all." There was no reason to upset Shannon by telling her that the children's grandparents had already filed the lawsuit, Mitch decided. After all, it was his problem, not Shannon's.

But his voice had been sharper than he'd intended, and he softened the impact with a smile. "Everything's under control, angel. Don't worry about a thing."

Hoping to brighten Mitch's somber mood, Shannon allowed her gaze to wander across the bulletin board papered with Biff strips. "Are those the ones for next week?"

"Yes. See this date in the final square, right under the signature? That's the day it will appear in the newspaper."

Shannon studied the drawings. "Amazing. They look just like they do in the comics, only larger. You really are a very good artist, Mitch. Your characters are so realistic."

Mitch was obviously pleased by the praise and stood up, allowing her a better view of his work.

Following the storyboard, Shannon was perplexed. Since she'd met Mitch, she had made a habit of following Biff's adventures and had found the character becoming more sympathetic, displaying more honest human emotion. Obviously, that had merely been a temporary setback. As she perused the new strips, Shannon decided that Biff was returning to his shallow, chauvinistic ways. She was not pleased.

Mitch apparently hadn't noticed her frown of disapproval and motioned toward the bulletin board. "Well, what do you think?"

Shannon swallowed. "Well, it's, ah, quite amusing."

"But?"

"But . . . well . . . I guess I'm a bit disappointed in Biff."

Furrowing his forehead, Mitch squinted at the storyboard. "What do you mean, 'disappointed'?"

"I suppose I'm just a romantic at heart, but I kind of hoped he and Maggie would, you know, work it out."

"What makes you think that they won't?"

"Because Biff's ulterior motives are showing."

Surprised, Mitch blinked at Shannon, then stared back at the cartoons. "Biff doesn't *have* any ulterior motives."

Sadly, Shannon shook her head. Mitch had enough on his mind without her criticizing his livelihood. "Perhaps I've misunderstood." Pushing aside niggling doubts, she chided herself for reading too much into the antics of a purely imaginary character. It was only a cartoon, after all. Biff wasn't Mitch, was he? No, of course not.

She managed a smile. "It's really very funny, Mitch. I think Biff's fans will love it."

Mitch's breath slid out in a relieved sigh and Shannon realized just how much he'd needed that small bit of encouragement. Amazing as it seemed, the great Mitch Wheeler wasn't immune to an occasional lack of confidence. His vulnerability touched her.

"I'm so glad you're here," Mitch whispered, then pulled Shannon into his arms and softly kissed her throat. His lips were moving slowly upward when he stopped suddenly and sniffed the air. "What's that smell?"

"Oh, my God!" Shannon pulled away. "It's dinner, or what's left of it."

She dashed into the kitchen to find Dusty slouched at the table engrossed in a comic book. The pot of chili boiled and sputtered, coating the stove with its contents. A strange odor emanated from the oven. Moaning, Shannon grabbed the sticky pan, set it on a trivet, then whirled toward Dusty. "You were supposed to watch this for me."

Dusty looked surprised. "I did watch it."

"Why didn't you stir it to keep it from burning?"

Dusty's face puckered ominously. "You didn't say to stir it."

Frustrated, Shannon plucked a pot holder from the counter, yanked open the oven and retrieved the hot dogs. She saw Mitch out of the corner of her eye.

He appeared horrified. "What was *that*?"

Shannon glanced down at the cookie sheet in her hand and saw the source of Mitch's shock.

So did Dusty. "How come they're all black and wrinkled?"

Shannon answered through tightly clamped teeth. "Just think of it as a new gourmet feast. Creole Blackened Weenies."

Mitch sputtered. *"Hot dogs?"*

Dusty nodded sympathetically, then gave Mitch a questioning look. Mitch responded with a curt nod. Dusty leaped from his chair and dashed from the room.

Shannon watched the exchange in confusion. "Where's he going?"

"To order a pizza," Mitch said, eyeing the charcoaled tubes, "and not a moment too soon."

Straightening her shoulders, Shannon dumped the hot dogs into the trash with as much dignity as she could muster.

Sensing that her feelings had been hurt, Mitch said, "Don't worry about it, honey. With a couple of lessons, you'll be cooking like a pro."

She stared at Mitch as though he'd just committed heresy. "I don't *want* to cook like a pro. I *hate* to cook."

"That's just because you haven't been properly motivated."

"And just what do you think could possibly motivate me to enjoy the smell of burning grease?"

A tiny smile pulled at his mouth. "As soon as the kids go to bed, you'll find out."

Chapter Eight

Mitch shoved the sticky pizza box into the trash, then nervously paced the length of the kitchen as the coffee perked. The children were asleep and Shannon was in the living room, waiting. This was it, Mitch decided. The big moment. Nothing was going to stop him this time.

He filled two cups with steaming coffee and walked quietly into the living room. Shannon was standing at the window, staring out wearing a distant, almost sad expression. When Mitch set the cups on the coffee table, the sound startled her. Smiling stiffly, she nervously smoothed her skirt, then turned back toward the window.

Suddenly Mitch had the overwhelming urge to touch her, to hold her. Slipping behind Shannon, he locked his arms around her waist, lowering his head until their cheeks touched. Their bodies molded together like matching puzzle pieces. "Umm...a perfect fit."

She fidgeted, then uttered an awkward laugh. "That's because we're nearly the same height. I've always felt like such a gargoyle, especially around tiny women."

"I'm not complaining. I've waited all my life for a woman who could look me in the eye."

The soft weight of her breasts rested on his forearms and she laid her head back, turning to rub her cheek against his shoulder. She felt pliable, soft and feminine, an arousing contrast to his muscled masculinity. He heard her chuckle, a low husky sound that raised goose bumps on his spine.

"Well, I can look you in the eye, all right," she said. "And in three-inch heels, I could check the way you part your hair."

"Unfortunately, Wheeler men aren't exactly basketball-player height. Ross is the tallest of the bunch and he just clears six feet."

Mitch felt her straighten slightly at the mention of Ross's name. A subtle change, but he noticed it. Last night Shannon had been quiet and withdrawn, and Mitch recalled that his brother had also seemed more stilted than usual. At the time, Mitch had chalked it up to concern for Rachel. Now he was beginning to wonder.

Mitch brushed his lips across her earlobe. "Is something wrong, honey?"

"No, nothing."

"Then why did you stiffen like a broomstick when I mentioned Ross?"

"Did I?"

"Uh-huh." His mouth found the tender flesh of her throat and he felt her shudder. "Now, what is it?"

Shannon chose her words with great care. "Your brother—well, he didn't seem particularly happy to meet me."

"Ross is never particularly happy. He used to be different. In fact, he was an incredible prankster as a kid and drove the girls crazy with his stunts." A thought struck Mitch and he laughed. "I remember one night my sister, Lauren, was having a slumber party. Ross squirted jelly in all the sleeping bags."

"Are we discussing the same Ross Wheeler?"

"He's changed."

"Apparently."

"When our folks were killed, Ross worked two jobs, managed to get his law degree and still made certain we all were fed, clothed and educated."

Shannon considered this. "You must be very grateful to him."

"I am. We all are. If it wasn't for Ross, the family would have been torn apart and shuffled to foster homes."

Suppressing a shudder at the thought, Shannon closed her eyes and leaned into Mitch's warmth. No wonder family meant so much to Mitch—and to Ross. They'd had to fight too hard to keep the Wheelers together. "I can see why Ross would feel so protective toward the children."

"It's even more than that. He has two children of his own who were the light of his life."

"I didn't even know that Ross was married."

"He's divorced. Although he has joint custody, his wife took off with his children. Ross has spent a fortune trying to find them, but he hasn't seen his kids in two years."

"Oh, my God!" Shannon whispered, unable to comprehend the pain of losing one's children. "How can he bear it?" Turning in the circle of Mitch's arms, she rested her cheek on his shoulder. So that was why Mitch felt such desperation about keeping the children close to him. He'd seen the devastation of his brother's loss.

A lot of things began to make sense now. Shannon had been bothered by Mitch's conflict with the children's grandparents, feeling that the Gilberts, too, had a right to know their daughter's children. She now had a better understanding of Mitch's desperation. The Wheeler family had seen too much loss already—their parents, their brother and sister-in-law, even Ross's children.

Lifting her face to Mitch, Shannon whispered, "There have been so many tragedies in your life. I'm very sorry."

"I just want you to understand, honey. It's important to me."

"I do understand." She snuggled against him and sighed contentedly. Enveloped in Mitch's arms, she felt warm and safe, as though she would never be cold or lonely again. The reassuring rhythm of his heart meshed with hers into a synchronized unison. Two hearts pulsing in perfect symmetry; two lives joining.

Shannon smiled at the poetry of her thoughts. A few weeks ago, she would have scoffed at such romantic nonsense.

That was before she'd met Mitch, before she had felt the power of his velvet touch. Even now, his fingers were stroking her shoulders, softly feathering over her spine, performing magic. And her entire body was responding to that magic. She was aware of a throbbing heat unfurling deep within her, a warmth that spread like melting butter from her limbs to her very core. Her bones seemed to dissolve, liquefied by the hot, satiny flow.

Mitch was whispering to her, soft words caressing like a gentle breeze. "You're so beautiful, my sweet. When you're in my arms like this, I feel as if my skin is suddenly too tight. You—you just take my breath away."

Joy surged through her. These weren't the words of a man preparing to end an uncomfortable relationship. All her worries had been for nothing and she felt massively relieved. She sighed. "I feel the same."

Mitch stiffened slightly. "You do?" His eyes widened and he looked like a puppy being offered a juicy tidbit, yet reluctant to take a bite. "You really do?"

Both surprised and amused by his stunned expression, Shannon said, "Yes, I really, really do."

She was even more surprised when he let out a whoop of delight, lifted her off the floor and swung her in a circle until their merging laughter bounced through the house and she squealed for mercy.

Finally Mitch stopped spinning, but didn't loosen his grip. His laughter died as his eyes darkened. Shannon's breath caught in her throat. Slowly, Mitch lowered his mouth to hers, nuzzling softly. Lips against lips, he whispered, "No mercy, honey, for either of us."

Then his mouth clung to hers in a kiss that was both deep and desperate. When her lips parted in a tiny gasp, he swallowed the small sound, tasting and savoring, coaxing her to follow until their flavors, like their scents, were mingled to form their own unique nectar.

The kiss ended, leaving them both hungry for more. Mitch groaned. "This is like walking barefoot over hot coals. I'm burning alive."

As he forced his hands to loosen their grip, Shannon felt him trembling with self-imposed restraint. Mitch tried a reassuring smile but it fell into a strained grimace. "I want you," he said helplessly. "And I'm about one kiss away from showing you just how much."

Shannon met his smoldering gaze, then lowered her eyes and turned away.

"Shannon?"

She recognized confusion in his voice and felt a twinge of guilt. Part of her wanted to run back into the safe circle of his arms and say "Yes, yes, yes." But another part of her was terrified. Shakily she crossed the room and perched rigidly on the edge of the sofa, as though prepared to bolt at the slightest provocation.

Watching, Mitch stood as though rooted in place. What had happened? he asked himself. Everything had been wonderful. Shannon had looked at him with melting eyes and wanting lips, only to stiffen and skitter away.

Had he frightened her somehow? Or had he misunderstood some subtle message? Fear iced his skin and he tried to calm himself, unconsciously rubbing the lump in his breast pocket. His palms dampened and chilled, his heart raced and his knees were dangerously weak.

Suddenly he was deathly afraid of losing her. It would be like a traumatic amputation, the loss of part of his soul. He couldn't let that happen.

Determined, Mitch gulped air, then strode unsteadily toward the sofa. "Shannon, I have something to—"

"Yeow-w-w-w-w!"

The cat leaped from under Mitch's foot, spitting and hissing.

Shannon gasped. "What was that?"

Mitch swore.

Caesar's ears were flattened.

When Mitch reached down, his gesture of concern was met by a low, rolling snarl. A paw flashed out. Mitch bellowed.

The furious animal dashed between Mitch's legs, then shot out of the room. Mitch eyed the nasty red streak on the back of his hand and muttered something about a recipe for cat soup.

"Are you all right?" she asked, smothering a smile.

Shrugging, Mitch slid onto the sofa beside her. "I'll live."

Lifting his damaged hand, Shannon gently touched the scratch and Mitch held his breath.

Quickly she released his hand as though afraid she'd hurt him, then looked away. The tension had returned.

Chewing her lower lip, Shannon seemed lost in thought and Mitch felt as though his Adam's apple had swelled to twice its normal size. He was acutely aware of the silence. The house was as still as a tomb. When Mitch cleared his throat, the sound echoed.

"Shannon, I've been trying to tell you—"

"I know what you're going to say, Mitch." Shannon reached for the cooling coffee and stared into the cup.

"Ah, you do?"

She nodded vehemently, unable to meet his eyes. "Of course. After all, we're both adults and there's no reason to beat around the bush, is there?"

"Well, no. I suppose not."

"You're a kind and gentle man, Mitch, and I've become very...fond of you. But—" The word caught in her throat, right next to the lump of fear.

Never in her life had she experienced such longing, such confusion. She wanted Mitch, but knew that for her, an affair wasn't the answer. Until this very moment, Shannon hadn't even known what she would say, hadn't dared face her own inner turmoil. She still couldn't face it.

Setting her cup on the coffee table, Shannon stood suddenly. "I should be leaving now."

"What?" Mitch's fingers convulsed around her hand, holding her where she stood. "You can't leave."

"It would be best if I did," she said simply.

Mitch stared at her for a moment, then slowly shook his head. "Somehow, I rather doubt that." He slid his palms to her cheeks, cupping her face tenderly, caressing her cheekbones with his thumb. He took a deep breath. "You're everything I've ever wanted in a woman, and more. I need you, and the children need you. Could you—I mean, would you—? Oh, hell."

Mitch stepped back, releasing Shannon and mumbling as he reached into the pocket of his slacks. With shaking fingers, he pulled out the small box and pressed it into her palm. "Open it," he urged.

Shannon stared at the velvety cube as though she'd never seen such a thing in her life. Her lips parted but no sound emerged and she looked up at him, her eyes wide with shock.

Impatient, Mitch said, "Let me." He lifted the hinged lid, displaying a brilliant, one-karat diamond solitaire. "Do you like it?"

"I-it's beautiful," she whispered in a very small voice.

Lifting the ring from its velvet nest, Mitch slid it on Shannon's finger, then sighed in relief. "It fits. I was afraid it would be too big. I told the woman at the jewelry store what lovely, slim fingers you have and she thought you'd probably wear this size." Mitch saw Shannon's pale face and frowned. "I knew it. You'd rather have emeralds." He muttered an oath. "We'll exchange it. You can choose anything you want, anything at all."

Bits and pieces of Mitch's statement seemed to have filtered into Shannon's dazed mind. She gaped at him. "It's the most beautiful ring I've ever seen but . . . it looks like an engagement ring."

Mitch's chin drooped. "It *is* an engagement ring. Shannon, I want you to marry me."

Her eyes widened first in shock, then in comprehension. "Marry? As in wedding?"

"Yes, Shannon."

"As in white lace and happily-ever-after?"

Smiling, Mitch nodded.

"As in what people do before they get divorced?"

Mitch's smile flattened. "I never thought of it in quite that way."

Staring at him, Shannon knew her jaw was sagging and she probably looked like a startled fish. She'd just spent uncountable hours worrying about every possibility concerning their relationship—except this one.

She started to chuckle. Mitch was gaping at her as though she'd suddenly gone mad. Desperately she tried to control herself.

It was hopeless. Some people cry when their innards are in turmoil; some merely faint. Shannon giggled.

Turning away, she clutched at her throat, trying to squeeze off the nervous hiccups, and her shoulders vibrated.

Mitch was bewildered. "Uh, does that mean yes?"

She nearly choked. "I—I'm sorry." Gasping once, she stammered, "I thought— Never mind."

"What did you think?"

Coughing, she wiped tears from her face and shook her head. Then Ross's image flashed in her mind. It sobered her.

All at once she was ice-cold. "What about the children?"

"They adore you." Mitch's eyes glowed softly. "Your first thought is always what's best for the children, isn't it? That's what makes you so wonderful."

Shannon's face flamed. Mitch had assumed that her suggestion was based on some saintly motivation. In reality, she was battling a sudden but deeply rooted fear of being rejected by the children. Shannon could still see Trudy's glum face when she'd discovered that her father and Shannon would be married. Trudy had seemed to change overnight from a cheerful, friendly little girl to an angry and tearful child.

Mitch seemed oblivious to Shannon's distress. "Think of it, honey. We'll spend our evenings together, our weekends together, we'll all be a real family."

"I—I have school at night. Mitch, I don't think—"

"Rachel and Dusty will be in school until noon." He frowned at Shannon's blank expression. "You could take classes in the morning instead of at night. Sis will watch Stefie for you." Mitch beamed, obviously delighted with his solution.

Eyes widening, Shannon felt her jaw go slack. "What about my job?"

"You don't need a job."

"Don't need—" She didn't hear that. In fact, this entire conversation had to be merely a figment of her imagination. At any moment she would wake up and laugh about it. "It's my father's business, Mitch. It's *my* business. It's what I do."

Pursing his lips, Mitch mulled this for a moment, then smiled and kissed the end of her nose. "Raising a family is more satisfying than soldering pipes." Shannon wasn't fooled by his teasing tone. Mitch was reorganizing her life right before her eyes.

"There's just so much going on right now, with the children's grandparents and everything—"

"Don't worry about the Gilberts. I'll handle it."

Seeing the quick flare of anger in Mitch's eyes, Shannon said, "They've filed the lawsuit, haven't they?"

Mitch's jaws clamped. "It doesn't matter. Once we're married, they'll have lost their only weapon against me."

Shannon turned white.

She could almost hear Ross saying, "I told you so." Oh, God. She couldn't handle this.

Mitch was talking happily, as though he hadn't just stabbed her in the heart. Turning away, Shannon stumbled toward the kitchen.

"What's wrong?" Mitch followed, instantly alarmed. "Shannon, what is it?"

"The coffee's ready," she mumbled, frantically searching for cups.

"We've already had coffee. Shannon—" Mitch captured her shoulders, turning her gently to face him "—don't you want to get married? Or is it that you just don't want to marry me?"

Seeing the hurt in Mitch's eyes brought Shannon out of her numb state. Reaching out, she laid her palm on his cheek and told him the truth. "There's no one else in this world that I'd rather marry."

His expression relaxed and he smiled. The smile froze on his face as she pressed the ring into his hand.

"I need time to think, Mitch. We both do."

Mitch's eyes clouded and his bleak expression tore at Shannon's heart. He rubbed at his forehead. "I've really blown it, haven't I? I didn't mean to rush you, Shannon. I've never done this before—"

"Shh." Shannon's fingertip touched his mouth. "Don't apologize, Mitch. You've offered me something beautiful and I'm so very honored. I just need some time."

Nodding, Mitch whispered, "Sure. I understand. Perhaps I should just, ah, go check on the kids."

After he left, Shannon sagged against the counter and closed her eyes, remembering Mitch's words: *Once we're married, the Gilberts will have lost their only weapon against me.*

She was also painfully aware that Mitch had said that he needed her, not that he loved her.

History was indeed repeating itself.

THE ADVENTURES OF BIFF BARNETT, PRIVATE INVESTIGATOR

Seated in a booth at the local greasy spoon, Biff and Maggie are grabbing a quick burger. Looking nervous, Biff says, "You know, I've been thinking."

Maggie grabs the ketchup. "That must have been a shock to your system."

Ignoring Maggie's comment, Biff reaches into his pocket. "I've been thinking about tying the old knot, Maggie. You know, the Big *M*. Whaddya say?"

"Why, Biff—" Maggie blushes "—this is so sudden."

Holding a sheet of paper entitled "Wife Application Form," Biff starts to read. "Can you cook? Do you own a vacuum cleaner? Is your car paid for? Does your mother live with you?"

Biff is now alone at the table. A wadded sheet of paper has been stuffed into his mouth and he silently wonders, "What'd I say?"

Pushing away the textbook, Shannon propped her elbows on the dining-room table and rested her chin on clasped hands. Studying seemed fruitless, since her mind kept rehashing last night's events.

For six years, Shannon had managed to fill her life with work, school and friends, her idealistic childhood dreams of home and family having been replaced by more realistic goals. At least a career was attainable—and it wouldn't break your heart.

Then, with a lopsided grin and twinkling amber eyes, Mitch Wheeler had swooped into her life, turning her safe existence into a tumultuous roller coaster of emotions.

Shannon felt as if she'd been sucked into a time tunnel. Mitch, like Robert, was a media magnet. And the woman by his side would, for better or for worse, share the celebrity spotlight. Both men seemed bent on molding Shannon to fit their needs; and of course, there were the children.

When Shannon looked at the men themselves, however, the resemblance stopped abruptly. Robert had been a cold man, distant and unfeeling, while Mitch was gentle, kind and generous. Robert was concerned with money and image; Mitch was concerned with people. There was one other difference, and it was significant.

Shannon now realized that she'd been infatuated with Robert; but she was in love with Mitch.

Closing her eyes, she pictured Mitch in her mind and smiled at that sweet image. He was so real she could feel the warmth of his body. With a devastating smile, he came closer, then closer still, until his mouth hovered inches from hers.

Mitch's lips brushed hers. She felt his breath, sweet and warm, as he murmured, "But I *do* love you, Shannon. I love you, I love you, I lov..." His voice drifted, as though he were floating away from her. Shannon reached out and grasped air. Then Mitch's voice disappeared completely, to be replaced by the melodic sound of bells.

Bells, bells, more bells.

Shannon jerked into a sitting position and realized that she was still at the table with her textbook lying open in front of her. Again the doorbell rang and she blinked, trying to focus sleep-heavy eyes.

Stumbling across the room, she looked through the small peephole, then opened the door.

Lindsay waltzed in. "Whatcha doing?" she asked, then tossed her burlap-sack purse on the table. "Studying, huh? Pity." Flopping on the sofa, Lindsay sprawled comfortably, then grinned. "I had high hopes that you would be heavily engrossed in something more exciting."

"Like what?"

"Oh, you know. Heavy breathing, groping in the dark, stuff like that."

Chuckling, Shannon shook her head. It was nearly impossible to be depressed with Lindsay around, and Shannon was glad to see her.

Lindsay's expression sobered. "You look like you just went three rounds without gloves."

"I guess I dozed off."

"I wonder why." Lindsay skimmed a glance at the book-strewn table.

Shannon wasn't up to one of Lindsay's lectures and changed the subject. "What brings you to my humble abode?"

Lindsay regarded Shannon for a moment. "Well, Frank called me this afternoon sounding like a lost puppy."

Shannon frowned. "Why?"

"Something about having rented some movie tapes and not having anyone to share them with. Apparently, since this is Saturday and you weren't there, he was feeling abandoned."

"Oh, swell," Shannon rubbed her eyes and sighed. "I haven't abandoned him, Linnie. He's my father and I'll always have time for him. It's just that finals are coming up, and, uh, I haven't had much time to study because..." Shannon's voice trailed off and Lindsay finished her sentence.

"Because you've finally established a healthy social life, and more power to you. But time is not a limitless commodity. You're already tapped to the max." Lindsay thumped her finger on the coffee table for emphasis. "Something will have to go."

"I'll manage." Shannon's chin lifted stubbornly. "I prefer to keep busy."

"Oh, for crying out loud, Shannon. There's a big difference between keeping busy and killing yourself. Sooner or later, you're going to have to shift your priorities, and personally, I think Frank can learn to do his own laundry."

Folding her arms tightly, Shannon walked over to the window and stared at the street below. "I'm all Pop has, Linnie."

"I know, honey." Lindsay's voice was filled with compassion. "But now that you've met Mitch, you both need to let go a bit."

Shannon winced. "Maybe."

Lindsay squinted through her spectacles. "Want to talk about what's biting you?"

Whirling, Shannon looked into the sympathetic eyes of her best friend. Yes, she did want to talk but didn't know where to begin. How could she rationally discuss something she didn't even understand?

A mere twenty-four hours ago, Shannon had allowed her imagination to run roughshod over her common sense, alternately convincing herself that Mitch was either going to send her away or suggest some kind of bawdy affair. Never in her wildest dreams had she suspected that he would propose marriage.

But she should have.

Mitch needed a wife, pure and simple. And Shannon needed another marriage of convenience as badly as Snyder needed more fleas. It was logical—no, it was imperative that Shannon run from this impossible situation as though her life depended on it.

Her feet were on the starting block, the gun had sounded and Shannon was frozen in place. Why?

Because she loved Mitch so deeply that she simply couldn't bring herself to move, that was why. It was dangerous, it was foolish; but it was true.

Shannon was about to hold her burn-scarred heart over another proverbial flame. She couldn't help herself, and that scared the devil out of her.

Still, something flickered deep within her—a tiny spark of hope. Maybe, just maybe, things would work out.

Lindsay, bless her, intuitively seemed to understand Shannon's dilemma and sat quietly, waiting. Finally Shannon began to speak, relating the events of the past two days in a voice that shook and occasionally failed altogether.

When Shannon had finished, she felt drained.

After a moment of silence, Lindsay quietly asked, "What are you going to do?"

"I don't know. He made marriage sound so rational, like it was a perfectly logical solution, but..." Shannon shrugged helplessly.

"But you've already been through a marriage of convenience, right?"

Miserably, Shannon nodded. "I can't get what Ross told me out of my mind."

Lindsay snorted in disgust. "Ross Wheeler is a stuffed shirt and an interfering busybody."

"That's what I kept telling myself until last night." Shannon clamped her lips together. She hadn't told Lindsay what Mitch had said about the Gilberts. Somehow she simply couldn't bear to feel the words in her mouth. Finally she whispered, "Lindsay, I'm so frightened."

"*What* are you frightened of?"

"Of making another mistake, of failing again."

"*You* didn't fail the first time, Shannon. Robert coerced you into marriage on a false premise. He never loved you."

Shannon sucked in a sharp breath. Lindsay couldn't know that her words had struck home. Shannon hadn't mentioned that Mitch, too, had avoided the word *love*.

Standing, Lindsay walked over and hugged Shannon. "There are no guarantees in life, kiddo. All you can do is follow your heart and hope for the best."

The simplicity of Lindsay's wisdom startled Shannon. The only certainty in Shannon's heart was her love for Mitch. But could a lifetime commitment be built on the weak foundation of a one-sided love?

Maybe. The tiny flicker of hope flared brighter.

A little voice echoed in her mind and she remembered Mitch's eyes glowing with sweetness, the soft sound of his husky whispers as he held her. This was a man who cared— and cared deeply. He was the man Shannon loved.

Her spine stiffened with determination. Yes, it could work between them. She would make it work.

Lindsay snapped her fingers in front of Shannon's face. "Hello in there."

"Umm?" Shannon reined in her thoughts and tried to focus on Lindsay's words. "What did you say?"

"I said, how about taking the night off and painting the town with your best and dearest friend?"

"Paint the town?"

"Sure. It's only four o'clock. We've got time to buy out that pricey boutique at the mall and then we'll dine on exquisite cuisine at Ambrosia Continental. I'm ready when you are.''

Shannon's gaze skimmed Lindsay. As usual, her attire was unique. "I doubt if that outfit will meet the dress code.''

"What's wrong with my clothes? White-washed denim is very chic.''

"Yes, but the jacket has frayed holes where the arms should be and the hat would look more at home on an Australian bush-pilot.''

Lindsay's nose wrinkled. "Picky, picky. Okay. How about a burger at the chili house?''

Smiling, Shannon shook her head. She didn't want to hurt Lindsay's feelings, but she really needed some time alone tonight. Gesturing toward the cluttered table, Shannon said, "I've still got a ton of reading to do this evening. I'll see you Monday, okay?''

"Whoa. You don't have to hit me with a bag of bricks. I know when I've been told to buzz off.''

"Oh, Linnie—''

"No problem.'' Lindsay grinned, punctuated her words with a cheery wave and disappeared out the front door.

Mitch sat at his drawing table, staring into thin air.

Over the weekend, he had come to some startling revelations. Although Mitch hadn't expected Shannon simply to fall into his arms, sobbing in gratitude at the prospect of being his wife, he hadn't been prepared for her shocked expression, either.

Thinking back over the past weeks, Mitch realized that he'd never really courted Shannon—flowers, champagne, romantic late-night suppers, that sort of thing. He'd simply seen her, decided that she would be perfect for him and perfect for the children, then blithely informed her of that fact.

Proposing marriage was something Mitch didn't do every day. In fact, he'd *never* done it; and if the truth be known, he'd never even considered it. Then, when he found the woman of his dreams, he screwed the whole thing up by

shoving a ring on her finger with all the delicacy of a gorilla in heat.

No doubt about it, Mitch decided bleakly. He'd blown it.

Shannon deserved soft lights and sweet romance, and that
was exactly what Mitch planned to give her. That, and the
time she'd requested. He wouldn't rush her or run roughshod over her feelings.

But he wouldn't give up, either.

"Uncle Mitch?" Dusty was peeking cautiously through
the doorway.

"Umm? Hi, sport. Come on in."

Dusty shuffled into the room. Reaching Mitch's work
area, Dusty shifted uncomfortably and studied the carpet.

"What's on your mind, Dusty?"

A listless shrug. "I was just wondering, that's all."

Mitch swallowed his annoyance. "Wondering about
what?"

"Things."

Mitch's patience, such as it was, was nearly worn
through. "I don't have time for this right now, Dusty. If you
have something to say, spit it out. Otherwise—"

Suddenly Mitch saw Dusty's puckered expression and realized how he must have sounded. What had been wrong
with him lately? Mitch knew that he'd been impatient with
the children, surly with his business associates and downright nasty to the world in general. Sure, he had one or two
problems at the moment, but who didn't? Mitch didn't like
to think that he was the type to wilt under pressure. That
would reveal a significant character flaw, and it wasn't, well,
manly.

"I'm sorry, Dusty." He pulled the boy into his lap,
smoothing his hair. "Now, what was it you wanted to say?"

"Are you going to send us away?" Dusty's voice cracked
and his eyes flooded.

Mitch's jaw fell open. "Of course not! Where in the
world did you get such an idea?"

"I dunno. You don't go to soccer with me anymore and
you send us to Aunt JoAnn when we're bad—" Dusty

gulped air ''—and you're always whispering about Grandma and Grandpa and then you play your oboe and . . . everything.''

Mitch could only stare. He'd deliberately kept his problems from the children because he hadn't wanted to worry them. He could see now what a mistake that had been. Dusty had known that something was wrong, but unarmed with facts, the child had nothing but fears. Mitch realized that he'd done the same thing with Shannon—refusing to share his concerns, refusing to communicate.

Had she, like Dusty, misread Mitch's actions? What was Shannon thinking? What was she feeling? Mitch didn't know, and the realization shocked him. He'd never asked her, just as he'd never asked what she wanted. Mitch had always assumed that her goals were the same as his, but he'd never, ever, asked her.

With a groan, Mitch scooped Dusty into his arms. ''Okay, sport, it's time to talk.''

Mitch and Dusty spent nearly an hour together. The boy's capacity to grasp the situation's complexities surprised Mitch. In the end, Dusty accepted his uncle's explanation and even seemed relieved. Reality, it seemed, was far kinder than the boy's tormented fantasies.

A much happier child hugged Mitch and scampered from the room. Mitch, however, had had little chance to digest what he'd just learned, when Ross's voice filtered into the study. Walking to the doorway, Mitch saw his brother toss a laughing Dusty into the air.

''Again, Uncle Ross,'' the boy pleaded. ''Higher.''

''Any higher, Dustin, and you'll have a nosebleed.'' Ross ruffled Dusty's hair and lowered him to his feet. ''Now, off with you. I have to talk to Uncle Mitch.''

''Can't we play checkers first? I'm getting real good.''

''I'm sure you are.'' Ross squatted until he was at eye level with his nephew and gave him a fervent hug. ''How about later tonight?''

''Okay.'' With a bright grin, Dusty bounded up the stairs.

Ross strode into the study and Mitch saw that his brother's smile had been replaced by guarded eyes and a somber frown. "I assume from your sour expression that this isn't a social visit."

"No, it's not." Ross laid his briefcase on the desk. "Now that the Gilberts have officially filed a petition with the court, there will be some unpleasant ramifications."

"Such as?"

"Such as a social services investigation on both sides of the issue. I can assure you that they will be quite thorough."

"Exactly what are you trying to say—that they'll interview anyone who's ever said three words to me, make a scrapbook out of every article that's even mentioned my name and examine every aspect of my moral character?" Mitch speared his fingers through his hair. "Tell me something I don't already know."

Ross's lips thinned and he didn't meet Mitch's eyes. "Have you, ah, discussed that personal matter with Ms. Doherty?"

"I asked Shannon to marry me, if that's what you mean."

Nodding, Ross stared at the carpet and frowned. "You are aware, of course, that her background will be of considerable interest to the child-welfare investigators."

Shrugging, Mitch maintained a neutral expression. Subconsciously he *had* realized that, but simply hadn't considered it to be a problem.

Clasping his hands behind his back, Ross looked up.

His brother's hard expression chilled Mitch to the bone. "Good grief, Ross, you look like you're about to do battle with the Grim Reaper."

"That might be a more pleasant alternative."

"Alternative to what?"

"To what I'm about to tell you."

Mitch tensed but kept his expression bland. "I'm listening."

Ross opened his briefcase, fidgeted with the neatly nested files as though stalling for time, then emitted a resigned sigh. He closed the case with a snap. "It's about Ms. Doherty."

"What about Shannon?" Mitch's eyes narrowed dangerously and he stood reflexively.

"Sit down, Mitchell. You're not going to like this."

Chapter Nine

As Shannon sorted the day's work orders, her kinked muscles howled for the solace of a hot shower. Glancing at her watch, she cringed at the late hour and piled the remaining papers into a rumpled stack.

The door of her office flew open and Mitch strode in. He closed the door behind him and stared at Shannon with numb eyes.

Shannon was instantly alarmed. "Mitch, what is it?" A horrible thought struck her and she bolted from her chair. "Rachel—?"

"Rachel's fine." The words were clipped and harsh.

"Then what's wrong?" Shannon asked, bewildered.

Standing rigidly in the center of the room, Mitch regarded her with cool detachment, but Shannon could feel the undercurrent of anger. When he spoke, his voice was so soft she could barely make out the words. "Is it true?"

"Is what true?" She felt a chill. "I don't understand."

He ignored her question. "Tell me about your marriage, Shannon."

Shaking her head in confusion, she said, "I *did* tell you about it."

"But you neglected to mention that your ex-husband is Robert Willis, a multimillionaire of questionable virtue with financial fingers in everything from Manhattan real estate to Las Vegas casinos." Mitch's jaw clenched and his eyes impaled her. "You also neglected to mention that the divorce was a media event."

Shannon was suddenly cold; cold to the bone. "I didn't think the details would be important to you."

"Not important?" Pain radiated from his eyes. "You deceived me, Shannon."

"You can't honestly believe that." Shannon couldn't bear to see the accusation in his eyes, and turned away. She felt ill.

This must be a nightmare, she told herself. At any moment she would wake up and discover that this moment was all just a horrible dream.

The room seemed to spin, and trying to focus on the hanging bookshelf in front of her, she clutched it with both hands. Her fingertips curled over the flat wooden edge, supporting her sagging weight. She felt as if she were dangling over a precipice.

In a way, she was.

Slumping forward, she rested her head on her knuckles. Behind her, Mitch was silent. Then Shannon heard a husky whisper and recognized the sound of her own voice. "I don't understand any of this."

She heard movement, agitated pacing and the sound of air being forcefully sucked in and expelled.

"What is it you want to know?" she asked numbly.

Mitch's voice was ragged. "The truth."

"The truth?" Shannon's head wobbled up and her neck felt like limp spaghetti, but she managed to look at Mitch. His eyes were dark and hollow. What was this awful "truth"? she wondered. Did he think she was some kind of ax murderess?

Her paralysis was replaced by a deep, tingling anger. "I don't know what you're expecting to hear. I suspect you'll find it all rather dull and disappointing, but here goes." Her eyes snapped. "I was nineteen when I met Robert. I was flattered by his attention and I adored his nine-year-old daughter, Trudy. After the wedding, Trudy saw me as a rival and became jealous. Normal behavior, of course, but I was too inexperienced with children to handle it properly. Am I going too fast for you?"

Releasing her grip on the shelf, Shannon felt unwelcome moisture gather on her lashes and angrily brushed it away. From the corner of her eye, she saw Mitch take a step toward her and quelled him with a sharp look. Words rushed out in a torrent. "Eventually, Robert told me that he'd only married me because Trudy needed a mother, and since I obviously couldn't handle the job, he wanted a divorce. It hit the papers, we settled out of court, end of story." Shannon took a deep breath. "There's your truth, Mitch. Was it up to your expectations?"

Mitch looked surprised. "What do you mean?"

"Obviously, you were hoping for something sinister. Did you get some kind of anonymous tip or do you use paid informants?"

"That's not funny."

"It wasn't meant to be. Where did you get your information?"

Plowing stiff fingers through his hair, Mitch looked away. "As my attorney, Ross felt obligated to investigate anything that could have an effect on the custody case. When he found out I wanted to marry you..." His voice trailed off.

"Ah, yes. The great Ross Wheeler strikes again. This is rather like applying for a security clearance, isn't it? Was I to be fingerprinted as well?"

"That's ridiculous."

"Is it? My marriage was a mistake, Mitch. That doesn't make me a criminal."

"Of course it doesn't," Mitch said in frustration. "That's not the point."

"Just what *is* the point of all this? Please enlighten me."

"No judge in the world will give me custody if—" The impact of his own words hit him.

Shannon's lungs seemed to collapse and her hand clutched at her abdomen as though she were in terrible pain.

Hurriedly, Mitch tried to repair the damage. "I don't mean that the way it sounds."

"Of course, you do." Shannon felt the room sway again and steadied herself by touching the desk. Her worst fears had just been confirmed and she felt ill. "Where there's smoke, there's fire, right? Besides, why take chances? After all, you only wanted to marry me to increase your odds in court." Shannon's breath was irregular, ragged. She was shaking all over and couldn't seem to get enough air. "Ross tried to warn me, but I was too stubborn to listen."

"Ross? What has Ross got to do with this?"

Ignoring Mitch's question, Shannon emitted a dry laugh that sounded like a strangled sob. "What an idiot I was to think there was any hope for us. You've dismissed my career as unimportant, treated my educational goals like a harmless hobby and all the time you were looking for—for some kind of weapon."

Shocked by her words, Mitch froze like a grim statue.

The pain was too deep for tears. Her eyes were hot and dry. They bored into Mitch. "Too bad you forgot the Wife Application Form. Maybe your alter ego can get an extra copy for your next candidate."

Grabbing her purse, she stumbled toward the door. As she passed Mitch, he seemed to come out of his shocked stupor and reached toward her. "Shannon, wait. We have to talk."

Shrugging him off, she looked over her shoulder. "I—I *cared* for you. Who deceived whom, Mitch?"

Then she went out the door, leaving Mitch shaken and cold, haunted by the memory of his own damning words.

* * *

Moonlight sprayed through the venetian blinds, casting dim stripes against the midnight blackness of the room. In the shroud of darkness, Mitch listened to the reverberating rhythm of a ticking clock and sought relief from his mental torment.

Staring at the fuzzy light slashes on the wall, Mitch felt as empty as the whiskey glass rolling between his palms. It had been two days since he'd confronted Shannon. Two days and what seemed like a hundred nights.

At first he'd been stunned by her accusation, then angry. But as hours had crawled into days, memories clung to him like annoying insects until, finally, he could no longer ignore their sting.

Raising a family is more satisfying than soldering pipes. Once we're married, they'll have lost their only weapon against me. No judge in the world will give me custody if—

But there were other memories, tender memories of her softness as she melted against him, of her sweet fragrance and the way her eyes darkened with longing.

In some ways, Shannon had been right about him. Mitch realized that his every action had confirmed her deepest fears. From the moment he'd watched her comfort Dusty with gentle compassion, Mitch had pursued her with a single burning thought—to create the perfect family. It was as though he'd needed to recreate the loving environment of his own youth, to complete the cycle that had been broken by the death of his own parents.

Mitch had seen Shannon not as the independent and successful woman that she was, but as an extension of his own dreams. He'd tried to change her and mold her into his own vision of perfection.

At the time, Mitch hadn't consciously understood his own motives but he now accepted that he'd been wrong—terribly, hurtfully wrong. He realized that now, so why couldn't he simply pick himself up and move on? Heaven knows, he'd done just that often enough over the years. In the past, when Mitch had discovered that a woman who'd interested him had conflicting goals, he'd simply shrugged and moved on.

This was different. What Mitch was feeling was unique, an emotional intensity that was totally new, completely unexpected and—this was the scary part—uncontrollable.

As his brain pondered a logical explanation, Mitch's heart supplied the simple answer. Somewhere along the way, Mitch Wheeler had fallen in love.

THE ADVENTURES OF BIFF BARNETT, PRIVATE INVESTIGATOR

It's late at night. Biff is walking down a deserted street when Willie the Weasel steps from a dark alley and jabs a gun into Biff's ribs. "You snatched my snitch, Barnett," growls Weasel. "I'm gonna do time, sucker, but you're gonna do life."

Lieutenant Maggie Kramer suddenly appears and aims her weapon at the mobster's back. "Freeze, Weasel!"

Biff grabs Weasel's gun and they struggle. The revolver fires, striking Maggie.

Dropping to his knees, Biff gathers Maggie's limp body into his arms. "Don't die on me, baby! I—I love you."

Pulling in front of the jobsite, Mitch saw the old frame house was in the throes of massive renovation. The property appeared to be under siege as a platoon of contractors pounded, drilled, sawed and hammered at the helpless structure. A steady stream of plaster-dusted workers watched curiously as Mitch tentatively neared the porch and peered through the open front door.

It had taken half the morning for Mitch to convince Frank Doherty that he absolutely *had* to see Shannon. Mitch had alternately begged and threatened, but Doherty had simply glared and given a colorful suggestion as to what Mitch could do with the rest of the day.

Finally Mitch had swallowed his pride, nearly choked on his ego and told Frank everything. And Frank Doherty had listened as Mitch poured out his heart and opened his soul.

How long Mitch had loved Shannon, he honestly couldn't say, but he certainly loved her now. It made a deep ache in his heart, a profound joy mingled with pain that was driving him to the brink of a kind of sweet insanity. It was like nothing Mitch had ever experienced in his life; and the feeling was frightening, yet strangely soothing.

It was love.

Frank had wiped damp eyes, scrawled an address on a scrap of paper, then growled, "Tell it to Shannon."

Mitch planned to do just that.

With a determined expression, Mitch strode into the house and immediately tripped over an ill-placed stack of floor tiles. He grabbed at the wall to steady himself and a two-by-four crashed to the floor.

"Hey!" A burly man with a stool-studded apron glared at Mitch and a second man silenced his power drill long enough to give Mitch an indifferent glance before returning to his task.

Forcing a smile, Mitch brushed plaster dust from his sleeve and said, "Where's Sha—" The shriek of a nearby buzz saw drowned out the remainder of his question.

The aproned man squinted, cupped his ear with a beefy palm and mouthed the word "Who?"

With a deep breath, Mitch yelled, "Doherty! A-1 Plumbing!" He was rewarded by a nod and the man gestured toward a doorway on the far side of the room.

Carefully stepping over wood scraps and broken plaster, Mitch worked his way toward the kitchen. The area seemed to have been gutted. Ceiling tiles had been removed, exposing a maze of chrome tubes and colored wire bundles. The floor was cluttered with scattered tools, debris and a large cast-iron sink that was propped against the far wall.

The counters were covered with white dust and there was a gaping hole where the sink should have been. But it was the open cupboard beneath the opening that captured Mitch's attention.

Two long, slender legs clad in familiar blue cotton extended from the cupboard under the sink opening. A slim hand snaked out, blindly patted the floor, then grasped a wrench and disappeared back under the counter.

Mitch sighed in relief. He'd finally found her.

The relief was short-lived, however, and was instantly replaced by a sense of panic. Nervously he swallowed his anxiety and called her name.

His voice blended into a sudden burst of pounding, as though someone were trying to break through the roof with a sledge hammer. Picking his way through the clutter, he leaned on the counter, peered into the sink opening and stared into Shannon's startled face.

Even with grease smudged on her nose, she took his breath away.

He saw her eyes widen in surprise, then a myriad of emotions flickered through the green depths—shock, pain and confusion. Finally she turned her attention back to the pipe collar, clenching her jaw as she jerked the wrench. Mitch flinched, wondering if she was envisioning something besides a pipe in that metal vice—like his neck, perhaps.

Her lips moved and he leaned farther into the opening, trying to hear over the noise.

"What are you doing here?" she bluntly asked.

"We have to talk."

Shannon stopped twisting the wrench and stared up, swallowing the lump that had suddenly formed in her throat. Mitch looked like a Third World refugee. His eyes were bloodshot, his usually crisp clothes looked as though he'd been jogging in them, and it must have been days since a razor had touched his face. She fought the urge to lay her palm against his stubbled cheek and scolded herself for weakening.

With a determined push, she propelled herself out of the cupboard and levered to her feet. "In case you hadn't noticed, I'm working." She met his gaze. "Did Lindsay send you?"

"No. Your father told me where you'd be."

She emitted a sound of disbelief.

"I admit it took some time to convince him—"

"I'll bet." Turning away, she reached into her open toolbox and Mitch grasped her arm. She stared at the offending hand and he immediately released her.

"Shannon, pl—" The hammering resumed and Mitch raised his voice over the din. "I don't blame you for being angry."

Her eyes narrowed. "I'm so relieved."

"Please, just give me five minutes. Hear me out and then I'll go."

The back door flew open and a paint-spattered worker tromped into the kitchen balancing a ladder on his shoulder. "Heads up," he said cheerfully. The ladder swung around, Mitch wisely ducked and the man passed through the room.

When the ladder's final rung had disappeared, Mitch turned to see Shannon hoist the heavy enameled sink. Before he could move, she'd dropped it into the counter opening. Completely ignoring his presence, she began measuring the drain opening to the pipe below.

Mitch raked his hair. She wasn't making this easy. "Shannon—"

"Hand me that caulking gun."

"Umm?" Following her gaze, he saw a pointed tube nested in a strange metal contraption and handed it to her. "I *have* to talk to you."

"So talk," she answered blandly, then squeezed a thin bead of silicone under the shiny metal drain collar and seated it in place.

Frustrated, Mitch grasped her shoulders, whirled her around, then kissed her until her body went from rigid to pliable and he felt her hands slide to his neck.

When the kiss ended, she stumbled back and he saw tears brighten her eyes. "Now that you've gotten that out of your system, do you mind if I get back to work?"

"Yes, I *do* mind." The ceiling began to vibrate under another siege of pounding, and the shriek of a distant drill set his teeth on edge. He screamed over the noise. "I love you, Shannon. Can you hear me? *I love you!*"

The hammering ceased, the drill stopped buzzing and the entire house seemed to await Shannon's response. Mitch moaned and Shannon's cheeks were as red as apples.

Wrapping his fingers around her wrist, Mitch guided her past the grinning workmen, searching until he found an empty and somewhat private room—a small bathroom where he propped Shannon against the shower door and pinned her in place.

She closed her eyes and again wondered if this was some kind of illusion. Had he said he loved her? She heard hammering again and realized that this time it was the thudding of her heart. Although Mitch wasn't touching her, his mouth was inches from hers and she felt his breath on her cheek. This was no dream. It was real. *Mitch* was real.

She opened her eyes. "What you said...did you mean it?"

"I meant it," he replied quietly. "I don't really know when I fell in love with you. Maybe it was the first day I saw you or maybe it just grew, so softly and so sweetly that I didn't even realize what was happening. All I know is that it *did* happen and I'm in love with you."

Behind her, the frosted glass began to vibrate and Shannon knew she was shaking. "Last week, I would have given anything to hear those words, Mitch. But now...now it's too late."

"No." His voice was harsh and ragged. "Don't say that."

"I have to say it. Nothing has really changed. There are things in my life that are important to me—things I can't just toss aside to be what you want me to be."

She saw pain flash in his eyes, an expression of raw misery.

His voice shook with emotion. "I know you'll find this hard to believe, but I don't want you to change. Don't look at me like that, please." He took a deep breath, then plunged ahead. "At first all I could see were images from the past, the perfection of my memories. I thought we could recreate that environment, a traditional family unit that would be a tranquil island in a crazy world."

Shannon felt a surge of hope, then swallowed it, afraid of another disappointment. "You have a right to go after those dreams, even if I'm not the right person to share them."

"Oh, but you are."

Shaking her head, she said, "No. We're different people with different goals."

"I don't think our goals are so different. We both want a life filled with love and happiness and family."

"What about the children, Mitch? I love them, but in a way, they frighten me. There's so much to learn and such a high price for mistakes."

"We'll learn together, we'll work through our mistakes together."

"And the Gilberts? Will we face them together, too?"

Mitch's jaw tightened. "Yes."

"What if we lose?"

"We won't lose."

"You make it sound so simple."

"It is simple. It's as simple as two people loving each other." Mitch's voice broke and he blinked away a sudden rush of tears. Swallowing, he wiped at his face, then met Shannon's gaze with a silent question.

"Yes, Mitch," she whispered. "I love you, too."

"Catch it, Dusty. Don't run into the tree!"

Backing up, Shannon tightened her grip on the tiny toy football, then shot a perfect spiral pass toward the scampering youngster. Dusty reached out to snag the ball, then tucked it under his arm and dived over the chalk line that represented the backyard goalpost. Mitch had made a halfhearted effort to block the boy, then tripped and collapsed on the grass.

Shannon jumped up and down, clapping her hands together. "Way to go, Dusty."

Barking ecstatically, Snyder raced around the yard, then congratulated Dusty with a sloppy lick.

Mitch rolled over, sprawled on the lawn and said, "Foul. No score and fifteen yards' penalty."

"What?" screeched Dusty. Hands on his hips, he stormed over to Mitch and glared down at him. "It was fair and square, Uncle Mitch. You're trying to cheat."

Mitch's expression went totally innocent. "Cheat? Me? No way, sport. It's just that you forgot to kiss the football before you crossed the line." Faster than a blink, Mitch snatched Dusty and bench-pressed the laughing child. "Now, if you want the goal to count, you have to do three laps of the backyard, then bury a potato at midnight."

"Aw, come on."

"It's true. Ask Rachel."

Rachel had positioned herself a safe distance away and nodded solemnly in agreement.

"No fair. Rachel's on your team."

Shannon waded in among the flailing arms and plucked Dusty off of Mitch's chest. "I think we're going to have to let the referee settle this."

"The referee is upstairs taking a nap," Mitch pointed out, then turned toward Dusty and Rachel. "Why don't you two go see if Stefie's awake?"

"Okay," they chimed, then disappeared into the house.

Too late, Shannon noticed Mitch's lopsided grin and recognized the mischievous glint in his eye. Before she could react, she was on the ground tumbling in a tangle of arms and legs.

"You're just a rotten loser," Shannon said, and laughing, propelled herself on top of him.

He sputtered under the impact, feigning a malevolent glare. "So you want to play, huh?"

"Uh-uh." She tried to scoot backward but Mitch wrapped his arms around her, rolled over and pinned her beneath him. "Turnabout is only fair," he declared smoothly, running his fingers over her ribs.

Shannon's protest was muffled by laughter. "Stop! No, Mitch, please. I'm ticklish."

"Really? Even here?"

"Yes! Mitch!"

Suddenly his eyes darkened and Shannon saw his chest expand in a deep, ragged breath. She felt his muscles tense and his fingertips caressed her throat—silky strokes that warmed her to the bone. A low purring sound rolled from her chest and she wanted nothing more than to spend her life in the secure circle of Mitch's arms.

He brushed her forehead with his lips, hesitated, then skimmed slow delicate kisses from her temple to the corner of her mouth. The moist heat of his lips tortured her and she desperately wanted more. The children, however, would reappear at any moment and Shannon splayed her hands up against Mitch's chest. He looked down quizzically.

"You're squashing the air out of me," she mumbled.

Reluctantly, Mitch rolled over and pulled her closer. "Better?"

"Umm, much." Sighing, she snuggled into the crook of his arm and watched a wispy cloud float overhead.

Mitch pulled her closer and whispered, "Are you happy, Shannon?"

"'Happy' doesn't come close to describing how I feel." She sighed and snaked a slim arm over his chest. "I feel cherished. I feel like a cat curled up in the sunshine. I feel . . . something poking me in the back."

Turning his head, Mitch squinted at her. "Here, lift up and let me see." She complied and felt his hand slide beneath her. "Aha!" Triumphantly, Mitch held up a small stone.

Shannon chuckled. "My hero."

"Umm, don't heroes usually receive a reward?" Tracing the outline of her mouth, his fingertip tested the cushiony softness of her lower lip. He stared at it as though mesmerized, and his eyes darkened with desire.

Helpless, she felt immobilized by the intensity of his gaze. Moistening her lips, she started to remind him about the children.

She didn't have to. The back door flew open and Dusty hit the porch like a sandy-haired tornado. "Stefie's crying," he said, then gulped. "And Uncle Ross is here."

Moaning, Mitch rolled flat on his back and tossed his arms over his eyes. Anger washed over him like a hot wave. Today was Sunday and Mitch hadn't spoken to his brother since he'd learned about Ross's covert visit to Shannon.

At first Mitch had been shocked, not believing that even Ross would be so invasive. Eventually, though, small incidents had fallen into place and Mitch had accepted the truth; but he'd been too furious even to confront Ross.

Now it seemed that a confrontation was inevitable.

"Tell Uncle Ross— Never mind, I'll tell him myself." Mitch sat up glumly. He might as well get it over with.

Shannon had scrambled to her knees and was brushing dried leaves and blades of grass from her clothes. "Well," she said brightly. "You take Ross and I'll take the referee."

Nodding, Mitch managed a sexy smile. "We'll finish this later."

Shannon felt goose bumps at the implications of his promise.

Standing, Mitch helped Shannon to her feet. She brushed grass bits from the back of her pants, firmly refusing Mitch's enthusiastic offer of assistance.

His eyes traveled longingly over her hips, then he sighed regretfully and flashed a crooked grin. "Race you," he said, then leaped to the porch before Shannon could react to the challenge.

"Dusty is right," she called. "You *do* cheat." Shannon followed, bursting through the back door and skidding across the kitchen to snag Mitch's belt. Jockeying for position, they squeezed through the narrow doorway into the living room, laughing and declaring the race to be a tie.

Mitch's arm was wound around Shannon's shoulders and she felt his muscles tense. Looking up, she saw Mitch's smile die and followed his gaze to Ross, standing stiffly in the entry hall.

"Good afternoon, Mitchell," Ross said, then paused, pursing his lips as though considering the closing argument in a felony trial. "I hope you'll forgive the intrusion, but since you refuse to return my calls, I had little choice."

Mitch's jaw tightened and he continued to meet Ross's direct stare.

Shannon looked at the two men, stunned by the tension between them. The three days since Mitch had followed her to the jobsite had been beautiful, filled with laughter and hope. Not once during that time had Mitch given any indication that he had quarreled with Ross. In fact, Shannon now realized that Mitch hadn't mentioned his brother's name at all.

Feeling awkward and uncomfortable, Shannon tried to lighten the mood. "It's nice to see you again, Ross. Would you like some iced tea or coffee?"

Not allowing Ross to answer, Mitch said crisply, "Our business won't take long." Then he strode past his brother and went into his office.

Ross turned as though to follow, then paused and looked at Shannon. She saw hurt in his eyes, and sadness. Averting his gaze, Ross nodded politely to Shannon, then went into Mitch's office and closed the door.

Something was terribly wrong, Shannon realized, and wished she could shake the sinking feeling that she was somehow involved. Staring at the closed office door, Shannon brooded until a wail of protest reminded her that Stefie was waiting.

Hurrying upstairs, Shannon scooped the baby from her crib, showering her with hugs and wet kisses until the child's tears over abandonment turned into chortles of delight. Noting a certain dampness, Shannon found a box of disposable diapers. In spite of Stefie's giggling efforts to thwart the project, Shannon was successful and congratulated herself on wasting only two diapers in the attempt. Perhaps she was acquiring a knack for this mommy business after all.

Balancing Stefie on one hip, Shannon went downstairs and glanced around the living room. Something was missing, something that was at the moment, vital: the playpen.

Following the sound of childish voices filtering from the backyard, Shannon called out the kitchen window. ''Dusty, where does Uncle Mitch keep the playpen?''

''Umm, in the hall closet.''

''Thanks.'' Shifting the baby's wiggling weight, Shannon started back toward the entry hall, grunting as Stefie squealed and lurched backward. ''You are thirty pounds of trouble,'' she muttered, then set Stefie on the floor and began to search the closet. When the coveted playpen was located, Shannon dragged it to the living room and opened it. When she turned to get the baby, however, the hall was empty.

''Stefie?'' Shannon ran to check the closet. No baby. Calling her again, Shannon was becoming alarmed. After all, children can hurt themselves in a matter of seconds. A pudgy finger in a light socket, a poisonous cleaning liquid not stored out of reach, could spell disaster for a curious toddler.

Chewing her lip, Shannon turned her head and stared up the stairs, wondering how far Stefie could have crawled in thirty seconds. Then she heard the rhythmic thunk of tiny hands and knees on a wood floor. Following the sound, she saw Stefie outside the door of Mitch's office. When Shannon reached her, Stefie threw out her little arms and squeaked, ''Shaa-na.''

''Shh,'' Shannon whispered as she lifted the baby and turned to leave. Something stopped her. It was the sound of her own name.

Angry voices filtered from behind the closed door. Shannon's mind told her to leave, that whatever was going on between Ross and Mitch wasn't her business. But she heard Mitch's voice, low and deadly, and was frozen to the spot.

"You went to see Shannon," Mitch was saying, "and I want to know why."

There was a pause, then the sound of pacing footsteps. Ross spoke quietly, carefully. "I wanted to make certain that the young woman fully understood the situation in which she'd found herself."

"And just what situation was that?" Mitch bit off the words.

"I was concerned. I felt that Ms. Doherty was a victim in this matter, being in the wrong place at the wrong time. She's a beautiful woman, and from what I've learned about her, a sensitive one. She came into your life at a moment when you desperately needed someone, and I don't blame you for taking advantage of the situation."

Shannon felt her heart drop to her toes. No. Ross was wrong. He had to be. Shannon told herself that she was simply going to walk away and allow them their privacy.

But she didn't. She couldn't.

"Perhaps I overstepped my bounds, Mitchell, but I took the liberty of informing the lady what would be expected of her."

"Expected of her?" Mitch's voice grated like a dull buzz saw. "How in hell could you possibly know what I expect from the woman I love? Who left you in charge of my life?"

"You're overreacting, Mitchell. I—"

"Overreacting." There was a slam, like a fist hitting a desk. "You had no right to interfere with my personal life, no right at all. I've been patient with your pomposity, your holier-than-thou attitude and even your damned meddling, but this time you've gone too far."

Shannon could barely hear Ross's response. "I didn't realize you felt that way."

"No, you probably didn't because I never bothered to set you straight. Read my lips, Ross: *Butt out*. If you ever again dare to stick your nose into my personal business, I'll fire you as my attorney and disown you as my brother."

Ross's voice was stilted and heavy. "Apparently, I've misunderstood the situation. I apologize. I believed that retaining custody of the children was important to you, and my actions were directed solely toward attaining that goal.''

A chair creaked. "The children *are* important to me." Mitch sounded tired. "I love them and I desperately want to keep them with me. I want to watch them grow into fine, strong adults, and whether they're living with me or with their grandparents, I intend to do just that.''

Several seconds of silence followed, then Ross spoke quietly. "You really *do* love her.''

"More than anything in the world.''

"You realize that the Gilberts can use her background against you. And if they do, they'll probably win.''

"I know." Mitch said something garbled, then his voice strengthened. "Those kids will always be a part of my life, Ross, but Shannon *is* my life.''

Shannon couldn't stand to hear any more. Stumbling away from the door, everything seemed blurry and she realized that she was crying. Mitch had told her that her background wouldn't matter, that they would face the Gilberts together and win, but obviously that wasn't true and Mitch had known it.

Any doubts she'd had about Mitch's love had been totally erased. He *did* love her. He loved her enough to risk losing the children he adored, and the pain in his voice had ripped through her chest like a razor.

Shannon loved Mitch, so deeply that it actually hurt. She couldn't let him make such a sacrifice. There was too much at stake. For Mitch's sake and for the children's sake, Shannon knew what she'd have to do.

And it broke her heart.

Chapter Ten

Revving jet engines shrieked as giant planes lined the runway like a flock of great silver birds.

Frank Doherty shifted uncomfortably and transferred Shannon's carry-on luggage from one hand to another. He watched the bustle of airport activity and swallowed. "I wish you wouldn't do this, baby."

Shannon glanced at her father and blinked back tears. "I have to, Pop."

She saw him drag his gnarled knuckles across his face and her heart felt like lead. How could she leave?

How could she *not* leave?

Staying meant disaster for Mitch and for the children. To Mitch, the media had always been a friend, a tool of the trade. He couldn't realize the harm media gossip could wreak, particularly the type of public blitz that would pit a bona fide celebrity against two grieving grandparents and spice the entire mess with a twist of scandal.

But Shannon knew only too well.

Lessons from the past: would they haunt her forever?

Frank cleared his throat. "You've got a right to change your mind about marrying Wheeler. Why do you have to go away?"

"Finals are over and Mike can handle my work at the office. I just need a vacation, that's all."

That was hardly all. Without Shannon, the children might not be deprived of the only home they'd ever known or the uncle who loved them so dearly. They would all be all right. And Mitch, well, he would soon get on with his life.

And somehow, God willing, Shannon would find a way to get on with hers. But life without Mitch seemed an empty thing.

"If you want some time, baby, that's all right with me." Frank blinked rapidly, pretending to watch a 747 lift into the clouds. "I just don't want you to be running away from your problems."

"I'm not running away."

Of course she was. Her father suspected that a vacation had nothing to do with her decision to leave.

"Did you and Wheeler have a squabble or something?"

"No. I—I just realized I'm not ready for a serious relationship right now."

Frank's expression was skeptical. "Mighty sudden."

Forcing a light voice, Shannon said, "I guess you were right all along, Pop. You said I shouldn't get involved in another package deal."

"Maybe I was right and maybe I was wrong." Frank stared down at her. "Something is going on here, baby, and I don't like not knowing what it is."

Shannon looked away. How could she tell her father that she simply couldn't allow Mitch to give up the children because of her?

Mitch loved her. If he realized why she was leaving, Shannon knew that he would come after her, no matter what the cost. It was the most difficult thing she'd ever done, but she had to convince Mitch that she simply didn't love him.

Shannon was a lousy actress. If she tried to face Mitch, he would see through her lie. Then, if he touched her, she would shed the last vestige of courage and run sobbing into his arms.

There was too much at stake. Shannon could never build her own happiness on the rubble of someone else's dreams. Mitch would lose the children and would eventually resent that loss and resent Shannon, as well. Their love would die and Shannon wouldn't be able to bear it.

Pop would be alone, though, and that tore at Shannon. None of this had been her father's fault, and it was unfair that he had to suffer for her mistakes—again.

Sniffing, Shannon looked at her father and felt a swell of pride. Even though he would be left completely alone, he was standing by her, just as he'd done so many years before. Her heart ached to leave him.

A loudspeaker crackled, then announced a final boarding call for Shannon's flight. Frank's chest shuddered. "Guess it's time," he said dully.

Reaching into her purse, Shannon pressed a small sealed envelope into his hand. "Will you mail this for me?" she whispered, feeling hot moisture gather on her lashes. Just touching the hateful letter made her skin crawl. When Mitch read it, he would never want to see her again.

Frank nodded, then slid the envelope into his pocket. "Are you leaving because of me?" His voice broke. "Lindsay says I've been trying to keep you on a leash, taking advantage—I'll change, baby, I promise I will." He looked so wounded, so vulnerable. It seemed to Shannon that her father had aged ten years in the past two days.

Throwing her arms around his neck, she hugged Frank fiercely. "No, no. I just can't cause Mitch to lose the ch—" The impact of her admission hit her like a body blow. Loosening her grip, she managed a smile. "I mean, I won't be gone forever, you know."

His hollow expression said that he didn't believe that for a moment.

Neither did Shannon.

A ceramic pencil-holder crashed to the floor.

Slamming his fist on the drafting table, Mitch crumpled the letter. His head slumped forward as his hands tightened around the paper, crushing it as its contents had just crushed his dreams.

Shannon didn't love him.

Mitch couldn't believe it. He felt as though a knife had slashed into his stomach. When he'd received Shannon's note in this morning's mail, Mitch had been in shock. Desperately, he'd tried to call her, and when he'd received no answer, he'd called Frank Doherty.

Frank had confirmed the unthinkable. Shannon was gone.

In the shouting match that had ensued, Frank and Mitch had alternately blamed each other, then the telephone line had become quiet. Both men had suffered a terrible loss, and for a few moments they shared an unspoken empathy, a silent compassion for the other's pain.

When he hung up the telephone, Mitch felt numb. Perhaps Frank had been right; maybe Mitch had been to blame.

Over the past weeks, Mitch had made every mistake imaginable in their relationship. He'd subconsciously expected Shannon to give up her own life in order to share his, and now he realized that he'd been childishly jealous of Shannon's career and her educational goals. Mitch had deluded himself into believing that marriage would be a panacea for all of his problems and that Shannon would automatically mold herself into his own pie-baking image of domestic tranquillity.

There was something else that Mitch now realized. Mitch Wheeler, fully liberated modern male, had behaved like his own chauvinistic cartoon character. Using Biff had been a safe way to vent his own frustrations, his own insecurities.

Biff Barnett truly had been his alter ego; and this realization had shaken Mitch to his very core.

But he and Shannon had worked through those problems and Mitch had felt as if he had the world in the palm of his hand. The day Shannon had said that she loved him had been the happiest day of his life.

Obviously she'd lied about loving him. Why? To punish him?

Mitch flung the wadded note across the room. A bitter taste flooded his mouth. The agony of Shannon's betrayal mingled with the pain of her loss, tightening his chest until his breath caught in his throat.

A myriad of emotions assaulted Mitch—anger and hurt, bewilderment and fear. He suffered a physical and mental torment beyond his experience. But then, Mitch's heart had never been broken before.

The telephone jangled, an obnoxious sound that grated on Mitch's ears and set his teeth on edge. Slumping over the drafting table, Mitch dropped his head into his hands and counted the rings. He didn't want to talk to anyone right now.

Six rings, seven, eight. The caller wasn't going to give up.

It was probably Ross. Mitch had laid out a compromise plan and asked his brother to offer the Gilberts a settlement. If he didn't answer the phone, Ross would show up in person. In Mitch's present mood, that simply wasn't acceptable.

Mitch grabbed the phone and barked into the receiver.

"Wheeler?" It was Frank Doherty.

Swell. Mitch wasn't up to this. His jaw clamped. "Yeah."

A long silent moment. "I just remembered something Shannon told me before she left."

In spite of his sour mood, Mitch found himself straightening with interest. "What did she say?"

"Well, it doesn't make much sense to me. Might not mean a thing."

Mitch tightened his fingers on the receiver. He could actually sympathize with Frank. The man was alone now, completely alone. With his own large family, Mitch had never realized how protected he himself had been. He forced a gentle, encouraging tone. "I appreciate your call, Frank. What did Shannon tell you?"

"It was something about you losing something."

"Losing something?" Mitch pressed his fingertips to his aching forehead. Frank was right. That didn't make any sense. "Is that all?"

"Yeah. Said she didn't want to be the cause of you losing something. Does that mean anything to you?"

"No, not really—wait a minute." Something tickled the deepest recess of his brain and Mitch tried to pull it into focus. In his mind, he heard Ross's voice. Suddenly, the scene was clear as crystal. "Oh, my God," Mitch whispered. "The children."

Hanging up the telephone, Mitch stared into space.

She'd overheard his conversation with Ross. It all made sense now. Shannon was afraid that Mitch would lose custody of the children because of her.

Bending, Mitch scooped the crumpled letter from the floor, then dropped back onto the drafting stool. Carefully, he spread the wrinkled sheet, smoothing it with his palms. His fingers traced the curve of her signature, then he lifted the paper and inhaled the faint, familiar fragrance.

He nearly wept with relief.

Shannon *did* love him. She hadn't betrayed Mitch; she'd tried to protect him.

His surging joy was short-lived. Somehow, Mitch had to tell her how much he loved her and that no matter what happened, they'd face it together.

How could he possibly find her? Earlier, Frank had said that Shannon planned to rent a car and drive up the Atlantic coast. She could be anywhere. It would be impossible to locate her if she was constantly traveling and Mitch felt defeated by the immensity of the task.

Then an idea wiggled into Mitch's mind and he concentrated on the tiny spark, allowing it to blossom into a full-blown plan. There *was* someone who could find Shannon, someone who had access to every newspaper in the country.

Mitch's gaze fell on the storyboard over his drafting table. Biff Barnett had just gotten a new client.

Maine was green and beautiful, so different from Southern California's golden, sun-fried landscape. Shannon walked the shore of the small Moosehead Lake resort, alternately kicking pebbles and admiring the beauty of the land. The water was calm and blue, frilled by greenery and smothered with clean, quiet air.

In one way, the trip had been just what she needed. Without the comforting pressure of constant work, Shannon had been forced to allow her mind the access it had sought for so many years. A soul-search, some might call it. Shannon called it a life-search.

She'd always been too busy, *deliberately* too busy, to be a part of anyone's life—even Mitch's. Shannon realized that she'd been cowardly, avoiding commitment and with it, the pain of caring.

The torment she'd suffered in the past was a mere splinter compared to the devastation consuming her now. She felt an overwhelming sadness, a sense of loss so acute it was as though a piece of her soul had been ripped away.

But the knowledge that Mitch and the children would be together sustained her, helping her face each empty day. Their happiness was her only comfort.

Turning on the familiar path, Shannon hiked the route that had become second nature to her during the past two weeks. Around the gnarled cottonwood, second boulder on the left, then the clearing in which the old log restaurant would now be serving breakfast.

As Shannon settled into her favorite booth, the one with a spectacular lake view, she placed her order, and as was her newly formed habit, spread the morning newspaper on the table.

The waitress, a disgustingly cheerful morning person who reminded Shannon of Lindsay, filled her cup with steaming coffee. The day, thought Shannon as she sipped the rich brew, had officially begun.

Wistfully Shannon watched a blue jay dip gracefully under a pine bough and thought how much Pop would enjoy this beautiful area. She missed her father and had realized that if he'd been possessive and domineering, he'd received Shannon's unspoken permission to be that way. Over the years, she'd subconsciously used his behavior as an excuse to justify her own emotional isolation.

But that was before Mitch Wheeler had rolled into her life and captured her heart.

As her mind wandered toward Mitch, the image of his face filled her thoughts and Shannon felt the familiar, sweet ache in her heart begin. She loved him so. Again she fought an overwhelming urge to hop the next jet home. Maybe, by some miracle—

Shannon took another sip of coffee, then pushed the cup away. Miracles didn't happen in the real world. Mitch would have received the letter by now. He would be hurt, but she knew that hurt would soon turn to anger and eventually, to indifference. Mitch was a survivor. He would get on with his life and never want to see Shannon again.

Somehow, she would have to live with that.

Opening the newspaper, Shannon turned immediately to the comics. No matter where she'd traveled over the past two weeks, Shannon had made a point of following Biff Barnett's adventures. It was, she realized, a kind of mind link with Mitch. Now, as she scanned the page, her eyes widened in shock as she recognized a caricature of Mitch himself staring back at her.

She read the strip again and again and again. A wet stain darkened the paper and Shannon realized that she was crying.

THE ADVENTURES OF BIFF BARNETT,
PRIVATE INVESTIGATOR

Sitting in Biff's office is a familiar, round-eyed man with a conservative haircut. He gives Biff a photograph of a beautiful red-haired lady plumber. Biff whistles. "A real looker, Mr. Wheeler. Why did she take a powder?"

"She was trying to protect us. She just doesn't know how much I love her—how much we all love her." Mitch sadly hands Biff another picture, showing Rachel, Dusty and Stefie all looking as if their little hearts are about to break.

Biff moans. "Oh, no. Not kids again."

Mitch looks miserable. "She's the only woman I've ever loved. Please help me. I can't lose her."
Obviously touched by the poignant plea, Biff sniffs and says, "I've been there, man. It's tough."

Standing, Biff puts his hand on Mitch's shoulder. "I'll find your lady for you, Mr. Wheeler, and then I'll dance at your wedding."

Shannon flipped the car air conditioner to "high" and opened her collar another notch to take advantage of the cooling breeze. Los Angeles was sweltering through one of its famous July heat waves—a situation made even more intolerable by exhaust fumes and radiant heat from the pavement's sizzling surface.

Turning onto the familiar tree-lined street, she felt tension knot her muscles. Shannon pulled to the curb before she reached the house. Mitch's house. In spite of the midsummer heat, Shannon felt a chill that had nothing to do with air-conditioning. It was fear.

What if she was wrong?

What if she'd misunderstood Mitch's message?

Nervously she fingered the manila envelope, then opened the clasp and allowed the clippings to spill into her lap. One by one, she read them again, smiling. She wasn't wrong. Mitch Wheeler was far from subtle. Biff had spent the past three days canvasing the country in search of his client's redheaded lady plumber. The strip had become so popular that Shannon heard of a radio talk-show back East that had established a Biff hotline and was furiously logging clues on the mysterious lady's whereabouts.

A lump wedged in Shannon's throat as she slipped the clippings back into the envelope and summoned her courage.

After a few deep breaths, Shannon pushed the car door open, resolutely grabbed a bag from the passenger seat, and marched up the sidewalk. When she reached Mitch's front porch, she suffered a momentary relapse.

She should have called first, Shannon decided. It was rude to simply appear uninvited. Yes, that's what she would do. She'd go right back to her apartment and telephone.

Why was her finger pushing the doorbell?

Before she could answer herself, the door swung open.

"May I help you?" The sturdy woman eyed Shannon with a pleasant smile and suspicious eyes.

Momentarily speechless, Shannon could only stare. She was at the wrong house. Away less than three weeks and she had actually forgotten where Mitch lived. Her eyes darted around the familiar porch. She managed to find her voice. "I—I'm so sorry to have bothered you. I thought this was the, er, Wheeler residence."

The woman's smile widened. "This is the Wheeler residence. Is Mr. Wheeler expecting you?"

Shannon had been discreetly backing away preparing to turn and make a run for it. Now, she clutched the bag to her chest in confusion.

"Shannon!" Rachel squeezed into the doorway. "Shannon's here," she yelped, then bounded onto the porch as

Shannon dropped the bag and scooped the ecstatic youngster into her arms.

The next few minutes were a flurry of hugs and childish laughter. Dusty flew down the stairs and circled Shannon with whoops of delight and rapid-fire questions. Drawn by the excitement, Stefie toddled into the entry, clapped her fat hands together and promptly fell down.

"Stefie's learning to walk," Dusty announced.

"So I see." Shannon watched as the unfamiliar woman picked up the baby.

Rachel seemed to read Shannon's thoughts. "This is Mary. She keeps our house."

Laughing, the woman bounced Stefie against her ample bosom as Rachel primly completed the introductions, then Mary excused herself to put the baby down for a nap.

Shannon was stunned. "A housekeeper," she mumbled, more to herself than to the children. "I wonder why Mitch finally gave in and hired a housekeeper?"

A familiar male voice answered. "Maybe he finally grew up and realized that Superman belongs in the comics."

Shannon's knees wobbled. "Hello, Mitch."

"Hello, angel." He walked toward her, slowly, a bit unsteadily.

Shannon's eyes locked with his, pulling him with her mind, until he stood so close she could feel his breath on her cheek.

Mitch's voice trembled. "You got my message."

"The entire country got your message."

"But you're here."

"Yes." It was more a soft sigh than a word. She had so much to say. Why couldn't she speak? Because Mitch's arms were suddenly around her and he was murmuring sweet, wonderful things and she was holding on to him as though he were the only solid object in the universe. Her eyes were wet, but she was laughing. She saw tears shimmering on Mitch's face and pushed them away with her fingertips. "I've missed you," she said quietly.

Shannon felt a tug on her shirttail.

Solemn brown eyes gazed upward. "Did you miss me, too, Shannon?"

"Yes, Rachel, I missed you and Dusty and Stefie very much."

Rachel grinned. "And Snyder and Caesar, too?"

"Uh, well, I guess so." Shannon picked up the bag and rummaged its contents. "I brought you something."

It seemed like Christmas. There were picture books from Maine and Boston, tiny souvenir teacups commemorating the Boston Tea Party and a squishy red toy lobster for Rachel.

"Wow! Thanks, Shannon." Dusty settled on the floor, fascinated with the books. He studied a photograph of the Boston Harbor, then said, "Is this where Grandma and Grandpa live?"

Shannon didn't look at Mitch. "Yes, Dusty, it is."

"We get to go there next week," Dusty said. "For the whole rest of the summer."

Shannon blanched. Had Mitch lost the children, after all? Slanting a glance at Mitch, she noted that he didn't appear upset. In fact, he was smiling as though he didn't have a care in the world.

"Shannon?" Rachel was frowning up at her. "Didn't you get anything for Uncle Mitch?"

Mitch was startled. "Rachel, that's not a very nice thing to ask."

But Shannon dug back into her magic bag. "I hope it fits," she said, then laughed as Mitch held up his new Lennie the lobster T-shirt. "It's the real you," Shannon assured him.

Mitch eyed the shirt skeptically. "Is there some hidden meaning in the size of those pincers?"

"Claws," Shannon said. "Lobsters have claws, not pincers."

"Oh."

Dusty gathered his treasures. "Come on, Rae. I'll let you look at my picture books." The two youngsters disappeared up the stairs in a burst of energetic giggles.

Alone, Shannon and Mitch were timid and self-conscious. Shannon concentrated on folding and refolding the empty bag. Mitch fidgeted with the T-shirt and scuffed at the carpet with the toe of his shoe. The gesture was childlike and endearing. Shannon was touched by it.

"I, uh—" Mitch cleared his throat and tried again. "I have so much to say, I don't know where to begin."

Shannon nodded. "Me, too." Silence. "It's nice that the children are going to visit their grandparents." She held her breath.

Nodding, Mitch saw fear in her eyes and gathered her into his arms. "The battle's over, honey. Everyone won."

He felt her shudder against him. She spoke into his shoulder and the words were muffled. "I don't understand."

"It was pretty simple, actually. All I had to do was put my ego on hold and realize what was best for the children."

Stiffening, she snapped up and stared him in the eye. "You didn't give them up."

"No, we compromised on a joint-custody arrangement. The children will spend summers with their grandparents and they'll stay here during the school year."

Mitch brushed his lips over Shannon's forehead, remembering the tearful telephone conversation with Ruth. For the first time, Mitch had been able to truly understand the isolation the Gilberts had felt. First they'd had to deal with the grief of their daughter's death, then they were three thousand miles from their grandchildren.

"You understood, didn't you, Shannon?" Mitch's expression grew serious. "Those kids were being torn apart by the selfish struggles of people who were supposed to love them. And you tried to tell me, but I wouldn't listen."

Mitch's praise made Shannon uncomfortable and she felt the familiar heat creep up her throat. He gave her too much credit and she told him so.

Mitch, however, was adamant. "You understood what Ruth and Steven were going through, exiled from their grandchildren, still grieving for their only child. I was too wrapped up in myself to see it."

"You only wanted what was best for the children." She touched his cheek then, shocked at her boldness, quickly tried to withdraw her hand but Mitch captured it, holding her fingertips to his lips.

"I wanted what was best for me," he said sadly. "I have a lot to learn about love."

"So do I." She smiled nervously. "But I'm looking forward to the lessons."

Mitch's voice was a hoarse whisper. "Do you mean that you're willing to give me another chance?"

"We both deserve another chance. I've had time to do a lot of thinking, Mitch. I've taken a good hard look at myself and I haven't been too pleased by what I saw." She had to get this out, but it was difficult. Shannon turned and took a couple of steps to put space between them, to give her room to formulate her thoughts. "I've always thought of myself as an independent, self-sufficient woman. Nothing could be farther from the truth. I kept myself too busy to think, to busy to become involved with others, too busy to be hurt." She took a deep breath. "My defensive ploy backfired. I had no time for you, either."

"Shannon, no." Mitch couldn't stand it. "You have every right to pursue your life exactly as you wish to. I wanted you to give up everything to be with me, and I was wrong."

"Not entirely. You had a right to expect that I'd become part of your life, and I wanted to. I guess I was frightened. It all seemed too overwhelming, so intimidating." Shannon's voice dropped to a whisper. "Then there's Pop. He has his faults, but he's basically a good man. I shut him out of my life once. It hurt him terribly and I could never do that to him again.''

Mitch remembered Ruth's trembling voice on the telephone as she'd shared her feelings of loneliness. He saw the image of Frank Doherty, shaken yet proud, terrified of losing the daughter who was his world. ''Your father isn't going to be shut out of our lives.''

Overwhelmed, Mitch wrapped his arms around Shannon, hugging her so tightly he feared he might break her. ''Things are going to change, honey, I promise.''

''I'm going to change a few things myself.''

Mitch lifted his head, eyeing her warily. ''What, for instance.''

''School, for one thing.''

''You're not giving it up? Shannon, it means so much to you, you've worked so hard. Hell, you've only got another year to go. You're going to get that degree and turn A-1 Plumbing into a multimillion-dollar corporation.''

She laughed. ''That *is* the plan, but the world won't come to an end if I cut down the number of units I carry each semester.''

''It will take twice as long that way.''

''But I'll have twice as much time. What's more, I'll be taking classes two mornings a week. I'll still have to spend some evenings studying, but fewer courses means less work all around.''

''What about your job?''

''I'm not giving up my work. It means too much to me and to my father. Pop has agreed, however, to a thirty-two hour work week, which will allow two mornings free.'' She smiled brightly. ''Actually, it's all working out very nicely, don't you think?''

Mitch appeared stunned. ''I don't expect you to change for me—''

Placing her fingertips to his lips, Shannon silenced him. ''I'm not changing for you, Mitch, I'm changing for me. Besides, there's one thing that will never, ever change.''

"What's that?"

"I don't cook."

"I absolutely agree."

Shannon's eyes narrowed suspiciously. "Do you mean that you're willing to prepare three meals a day for a family of five?"

"Not at all," Mitch said cheerfully. "That's why I hired Mary."

"Oh, yes. Mary. Now that I've bared my soul to you, perhaps you'd care to enlighten me as to why you've broken your own cardinal rule about having strangers in the house."

Mitch shrugged and slipped his arm around Shannon's waist. "You're not the only one who knows how to compromise."

"I'll buy that." Shannon snuggled into the crook of Mitch's arm. "By the way, what's Mary's luncheon special? I'm absolutely starved."

Mitch stiffened, then coughed nervously. "Frozen lasagna," he muttered.

"What?" Shannon couldn't believe her ears. "Did you say *frozen*?"

"I'll have you know that you're talking to a thoroughly modern male, a truly liberated man." Mitch held up his hand, motioning for Shannon to wait, then strode down the hall into his study. When he returned he hesitantly took her hand, sliding the beautiful, familiar ring onto her finger. "We'll elope. No press, no family. Just you and me."

Shannon arched a brow in question. "Is that a request or an edict?"

Mitch looked crushed and Shannon couldn't maintain her indignant expression. She laughed.

"I guess old habits die hard," Mitch said. "Talk to me, Shannon. Tell me what you really want."

"You, Mitch. I want you."

As Mitch hugged her, Shannon wound her arms around his neck. Through happy tears, Shannon saw the ring shimmering on her hand. She could have sworn that diamond winked at her.

It was good to be home.

Epilogue

Sparkling with tinsel and ornaments, the Christmas tree twinkled while the Wheeler living room buzzed with merry laughter and happy holiday sounds. From the kitchen doorway, Shannon watched, wondering how it was possible to be so happy without absolutely bursting.

This was one of many family gatherings Mitch and Shannon had hosted during the four months of their marriage. Her contented gaze skimmed the sea of happy faces. She felt a small flutter in her womb, a joyful reminder that their family would soon be expanding.

Mitch had been right. Their life was perfect.

Shannon's attention was drawn toward Dusty, who was pulling a red-ribboned package from beneath the tree. ''Look, Stefie,'' Dusty said. ''This one's for you.''

''Pretty,'' Stefie said, then snatched the gift and hugged it to her fat tummy. ''Mine.''

''You can't open it,'' Rachel told her solemnly. ''Not until Christmas.''

''Mine,'' Stefie insisted.

"Yes, honey, it's yours." Mitch pried the package from her chubby fingers and replaced it under the tree. "But we have to wait until Santa Claus comes, then you can open it."

"Sa' Claus?"

Mitch bent to scoop the baby into his arms, then held her high over his head until he was rewarded by a squeal of delight. Mitch glanced toward a gaunt man, standing quiet and alone in the corner of the room. "Come on, Stefani," Mitch said. "Let's go see Poppa Frank."

Mitch swiveled through the humming throng until Stefie climbed happily into Frank Doherty's arms. Frank's face lit with pleasure.

"Are we still on for Sunday?" Mitch asked.

"Yep, but I've got to warn you, I'm feeling lucky." Frank kissed Stefie's cheek. "This time, Wheeler, I might just beat you."

Mitch frowned. "I wish my bowling skill was improving as quickly as your golf game."

Frank glanced across the room and grinned. "Well, now, just look at that."

Following Frank's gaze, Mitch saw Ross walking through the front door with Lindsay Prescott on his arm. "He looks ten years younger since he's been seeing Lindsay," Mitch said. "They say opposites attract, but I never would have believed that Ross could become entranced with such a free-spirited kind of woman."

"Lindsay is a tad different," Frank acknowledged. "But you know, I think old Ross has mellowed a bit. Why, he showed up at the office last week to take Lindsay to lunch and he was actually smiling."

Shannon could see Mitch laugh, but the remainder of the conversation was drowned by childish whoops of delight. She stepped aside as Dusty and two of his cousins ducked through the doorway and into the kitchen. Mary, who was busily preparing a second course of hors d'oeuvres, quickly dispelled the youngsters and they scampered into the backyard.

As the doorbell chimed, Shannon began to work her way toward the entry. She waved cheerfully at Mitch, who was weaving through the crowd from the opposite side of the room.

It was Shannon who opened the door. "Ruth! Steven!" she exclaimed amid a shower of hugs and kisses. "I'm so glad you could come."

"We couldn't resist an invitation to spend Christmas in the sunshine," Ruth said.

With a final hug, Shannon said, "It's so good to see you again. Mitch, could you please help them with their luggage?"

Mitch was pumping Steven Gilbert's hand with genuine enthusiasm. He answered Shannon's request with a grin and a nod, then grabbed two suitcases from the porch. "I'll take these up to your room."

As Mitch disappeared up the stairs, Rachel appeared and chirped, "Grandma! Grandpa!" Then she propelled herself into Ruth's arms. Shannon saw the older woman's tears as she covered Rachel's face with kisses.

Rachel wiggled down and tugged at Ruth's hand. "Come on, Grandma. Poppa Frank is here and you can meet him. He's neat."

At Rachel's insistence, the Gilberts followed. Shannon saw them pause at the threshold of the living room and hesitantly eye the crowd of strangers. Suddenly, Lindsay appeared and took Ruth's hands. Ross stood stiffly for a moment, then extended his hand to Steven. Soon the Gilberts were surrounded and Shannon saw Ruth look over her shoulder, eyes filled with gratitude and love as strangers became family.

Aware that Mitch had returned and was standing behind her, Shannon wiped her own cheeks. Mitch slipped his arm around her waist, holding her tightly against him. "I love you, Mrs. Wheeler," he whispered.

Shannon's response was drowned by a loud wail from the kitchen that was followed by a spurt of muttered oaths.

People moved in the living room, parting like a living sea as Snyder dashed through.

Mary appeared in the kitchen doorway, waving a wooden spoon as though it were a weapon. "That shaggy, four-footed sneak just ate my rumaki," Mary hollered. "I spent two hours wrapping bacon around those darn chicken livers and that...that..." Mary sputtered briefly then wiggled the spoon toward Snyder, who was peering from behind Mitch's legs. The dog whined as though contrite, then laid his whiskered chin on the floor. As a ripple of muffled laughter filtered through the living room, Mary tossed her arms in the air with a what's-the-use-gesture and flounced back into the kitchen.

Shannon tried to choke back a giggle. "I believe this is where I came in."

Mitch slid his hand over her abdomen, warming the tiny bulge with his palm. "I wouldn't have it any other way."

"Neither would I, my love." Sighing, Shannon closed her eyes, letting the happy sounds fill her mind and her heart.

Dreams really can come true.

THE ADVENTURES OF BIFF BARNETT, PRIVATE INVESTIGATOR

Having recovered from her wounds, Maggie is hard at work when Biff peeks into her office. "Hiya, babe. Working late?"

Maggie frowns. "Is it your night to fix dinner?" Seeing Biff's grin, she adds, "Then I'm working late."

Pulling a bottle of champagne from behind his back, Biff says, "Come on, Maggie, let's celebrate. It's exactly one month, four days and two hours since you dragged me down the aisle and made an honest man of me."

Maggie lifts an eyebrow. "Who dragged whom?"

"What's the difference?" Leaning over the desk, Biff flashes his sexiest grin. "I'm crazy about you, baby."

Maggie smiles.

*   *   *   *   *

COMING NEXT MONTH

#706 NEVER ON SUNDAE—Rita Rainville
A Diamond Jubilee Title!
Heather Brandon wanted to help women lose weight. But lean, hard Wade Mackenzie had different ideas. He wanted Heather to lose her heart—to him!

#707 DOMESTIC BLISS—Karen Leabo
By working as a maid, champion of women's rights Spencer Guthrie tried to prove he practiced what he preached. But could he convince tradition-minded Bonnie Chapman that he loved a woman like her?

#708 THE MARK OF ZORRO—Samantha Grey
Once conservative Sarah Wingate saw "the man in the mask" she couldn't keep her thoughts on co-worker Jeff Baxter. But then she learned he and Zorro were one and the same!

#709 A CHILD CALLED MATTHEW—Sara Grant
Laura Bryant was determined to find her long-lost son at any cost. Then she discovered the key to the mystery lay with Gareth Ryder, the man who had once broken her heart.

#710 TIGER BY THE TAIL—Pat Tracy
Sarah Burke had grown up among tyrants, so Lucas Rockworth's gentle demeanor drew her like a magnet. Soon, however, she learned her lamb roared like a lion!

#711 SEALED WITH A KISS—Joan Smith
Impetuous Jodie James was off with stuffy—but handsome!—Greg Edison to look for their missing brothers. Jodie knew they were a mismatched couple, but she was starting to believe the old adage that opposites attract....

AVAILABLE THIS MONTH:

#700 THE AMBASSADOR'S DAUGHTER
Brittany Young

#701 HIS CHARIOT AWAITS
Kasey Michaels

#702 BENEATH SIERRA SKIES
Shannon Gale

#703 A LIBERATED MAN
Diana Whitney

#704 SO EASY TO LOVE
Marcy Gray

#705 A PERFECT GENTLEMAN
Arlene James

Silhouette Romances®

DIAMOND JUBILEE CELEBRATION!

It's Silhouette Books' tenth anniversary, and what better way to celebrate than to toast *you*, our readers, for making it all possible. Each month in 1990, we'll present you with a DIAMOND JUBILEE Silhouette Romance written by an all-time favorite author!

Welcome the new year with *Ethan*—a LONG, TALL TEXANS book by Diana Palmer. February brings Brittany Young's *The Ambassador's Daughter*. Look for *Never on Sundae* by Rita Rainville in March, and in April you'll find *Harvey's Missing* by Peggy Webb. Victoria Glenn, Lucy Gordon, Annette Broadrick, Dixie Browning and many more have special gifts of love waiting for you with their DIAMOND JUBILEE Romances.

Be sure to look for the distinctive DIAMOND JUBILEE emblem, and share in Silhouette's celebration. Saying thanks has never been so romantic. . . .

SRJUB-1

At long last, the books you've been waiting for
by one of America's top romance authors!

DIANA PALMER

DUETS

Ten years ago Diana Palmer published her very first
romances. Powerful and dramatic, these gripping tales
of love are everything you have come to expect from
Diana Palmer.

In March, some of these titles will be available again in
DIANA PALMER DUETS—a special three-book collection. Each book will have two wonderful stories plus an
introduction by the author. You won't want to miss them!

Book 1
SWEET ENEMY
LOVE ON TRIAL

Book 2
STORM OVER THE LAKE
TO LOVE AND CHERISH

Book 3
IF WINTER COMES
NOW AND FOREVER

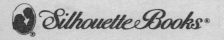 *Silhouette Books*®

DP-1